Quiz inside: Can you trust your boyfriend?

He was only supposed to be driving her to the beach. . . .

Suddenly they were kissing.

Liv's lips were soft and moist. Jeremy could feel the heat radiating from them. Tenderly he grazed her lips. He kissed her teasingly, playfully. Liv teased back. The kiss grew more and more intense. Jeremy's hands reached up and loosened her ponytail. A soft cascade of hair spilled out onto his fingers.

"Liv," he murmured, his hand moving down her back, pressing her even closer.

Without warning, Liv pulled away sharply. Her eyes were huge and wild.

"W-What are you doing?" She gasped, wiping the back of her hand roughly against her mouth. "Don't you ever do that again!" Liv said, her voice shaking. "What's wrong with you?"

She's Patrick's girlfriend. What have I done? Jeremy thought, his heart and his brain slamming into each other like some crazy dancers in a mosh pit.

The full force of what happened hit him.

He had just kissed his best friend's girlfriend—the one girl he couldn't have.

Don't miss any of the books in *Love Stories*
—the romantic series from Bantam Books!

My Best Friend's
Girlfriend

Wendy Loggia

BANTAM BOOKS
NEW YORK · TORONTO · LONDON · SYDNEY · AUCKLAND

RL 6, age 12 and up

MY BEST FRIEND'S GIRLFRIEND
A Bantam Book / July 1997

Produced by Daniel Weiss Associates, Inc.
33 West 17th Street
New York, NY 10011.
Cover photography by Michael Segal.

ISBN: 0-553-49214-4

Published simultaneously in the United States and Canada

Bantam Books are published by Bantam Books, a division of Bantam
Doubleday Dell Publishing Group, Inc. Its trademark, consisting of the
words "Bantam Books" and the portrayal of a rooster, is Registered in
U.S. Patent and Trademark Office and in other countries. Marca
Registrada. Bantam Books, 1540 Broadway, New York, New York 10036.

PRINTED IN THE UNITED STATES OF AMERICA

OPM   0 9 8 7 6 5 4 3

To Chris

ONE

SOMEHOW, SOMEWAY IT had finally arrived. And sixteen-year-old Jeremy Thomas was totally, completely ready for it.

"It" was the trip to the Jersey Shore that he'd been fantasizing about all summer long. Not only fantasizing about, but working for. Eight hours a day, five painful days a week, Jeremy had stocked shelves, bagged groceries, and reined in runaway shopping carts at Wegmans grocery store. If he had to unload one more carton of canned string beans, well . . . he'd lose it. Not that he didn't like carrying little old ladies' groceries to their cars and flirting with the girls in the bakery—but he wanted to have some real fun this summer.

After all, this was the summer before senior year.

Next summer he'd be getting ready for college. Life. All Jeremy wanted now was to kick back and relax. And that's just what was going to happen.

For years Jeremy had listened to his best friend, Patrick Clark, talk about Beach Haven, the New Jersey summer community where the Clarks spent July and August, and of Pelican's Cove, the family's summer beach house. It sounded like paradise to Jeremy . . . boating, swimming, excellent Boogie boarding and surfing. The beach stretched for miles . . . a beach filled with pretty girls in tiny bikinis, ready for summer fun and romance.

There had always been some reason or another that prevented Jeremy from going: Last summer he'd been mowing lawns and trimming hedges, the summer before that he'd volunteered at a camp for kids with cancer, the summer before *that* his family had been traveling through New England. . . .

This year the two weeks of August had dangled temptingly in front of his stock-boy weary eyes all summer. He'd thought they'd never get here.

But at long last, they had.

Jeremy eyed the pair of black Levi's that lay on his bed . . . next to the cream ones, the brown ones with the patches, and the three pairs of blue ones in various degrees of fade.

"Honey, you're only going to the shore for two weeks, not two months." Jeremy's mom hurried into his room, a pile of freshly washed underwear and socks in her arms. "I thought you might need these," she said, handing them over.

"Thanks." Jeremy sighed. "I just want to make sure I've got the right stuff."

Mrs. Thomas's eyes flickered over the bed.

"Definitely leave room for the underwear." She pursed her lips. "A couple pairs of shorts, some T-shirts, your swim trunks, and one nice outfit, and you'll be fine." Mrs. Thomas tapped her watch. "Better hurry, sweetie. That girl's expecting you at nine-thirty this morning, isn't she?"

"Yeah. She is," Jeremy said.

"Well, don't keep her waiting," Mrs. Thomas said, ruffling his wavy brown hair on the way out. "And breakfast's ready."

That girl. That girl was Liv Carlson. Patrick's new girlfriend. Actually she wasn't really all that new. Patrick had been seeing her for a few months. But Jeremy hadn't met her yet. *My best friend's girlfriend, and I don't even know her.*

Liv went to Lincoln High, while Patrick and Jeremy both went to Millcreek. Back in May, Millcreek and Lincoln had held a student council exchange day. Ten representatives from Millcreek went to Lincoln, and ten representatives from Lincoln spent the day at Millcreek. The official objective was: Learn about the other school, see what its classes were like, and bring back any inventive ideas to your own school. Of course that wasn't what really went on. What really happened was: You got the day off from school, everyone at the other school was dying to get to know you if you were attractive, and the only thing you wanted to bring back was a phone number.

If you were lucky. And Patrick was always lucky. Not only did junior-class president Patrick Clark

3

come back with some excellent fund-raiser ideas for next year's senior class trip, he came back with the prized possession of his seventeen years. The unlisted phone number of Lincoln High's most likely to wow, Liv Carlson.

Patrick had been raving about Liv ever since. At first Jeremy had been bothered by the whole deal. He was used to spending most of his free time hanging out with Patrick. Shooting hoops, rooting for the Pirates, playing video games in the Clarks' den, going out for pizza and wings. But when Liv came on the scene, Jeremy took a backseat. Jeremy had dated several girls, but he never put them before his friendship with Patrick. Girls came and went. They could never replace the guys he'd hung out with since forever.

This wasn't the first time Patrick had fallen for some girl. But by the way he talked, it sounded as if it might be the last. According to Patrick, Liv was the most breathtaking creature ever to step on United States soil. Patrick had wanted to introduce Liv to Jeremy, but it seemed like every time Liv was free, Jeremy was working. And when Jeremy was available, Liv was either with her friends or at her own part-time job at the mall. Somehow they just hadn't gotten around to meeting each other.

But that was about to change.

Jeremy smiled as he stuffed his black jeans and one pair of the blue into his suitcase. He and Patrick had been best friends for as long as he could remember. Jeremy could still recall the first day he'd met Patrick. The Thomases had just moved to Erie, Pennsylvania, from Pittsburgh, and Jeremy was in the middle of helping his dad unload what seemed like a million cardboard boxes, when a scruffy blond kid wearing a Pirates cap and madly pedaling a beat-up mountain bike came screeching into the driveway.

"Hey!" the kid had exclaimed, hopping off his bike. "I thought some old people were moving in here!"

"Well, uh, there's my parents," Jeremy had told him, gesturing to his dad. Mr. Thomas had poked his head from around a large shrub, a huge box in his arms.

"That's me. Resident old person," Mr. Thomas said, heading toward the house. He gave the kid a nod.

"But there's me and my brother, Mitchell," Jeremy finished. "Mitchell's inside. My name's Jeremy."

"I'm Patrick. See that big brick house down there?" Jeremy followed his pointing finger. "That's where I live. Come on! They're playing street hockey on the next block over!"

Jeremy looked up at the house and shook his head. "I don't think I can," he'd said ruefully. "My dad wants me to help unpack, and my bike is—" Jeremy stopped. Patrick had hopped off his bike and tore in the house.

Before Jeremy had time to think, Patrick was back.

"Your dad said it's okay! You can borrow one of my bikes—I've got three!" Sure enough, Mr. Thomas waved at Jeremy from inside. "Go have fun," he mouthed.

5

That was eight years ago. And Jeremy had been having fun with Patrick ever since. Patrick wasn't like other people. He was fearless. A born leader. So it was no surprise that when it came to girls, they fell for him big time.

Jeremy guessed that's probably how Olivia Carlson would be. When Patrick had asked him if he'd mind giving her a lift to the shore, he'd said yes without a moment's thought. He wasn't crazy about an eight-hour road trip with a stranger, but she couldn't be that bad if Patrick liked her. And although he was a little bummed that it wouldn't be just him and Patrick hanging out, he decided that wasn't all bad. It'd be nice to have some company.

At nine forty-five Jeremy finally pulled his red Celica up to 54 Rosewood Lane. The house was a sprawling brick ranch set back from the road, enclosed by a neatly trimmed hedge. A girl with long brown hair sat on the front steps. She stood up, hesitated for a second, and then waved.

"Jeremy?" she called tentatively.

Jeremy nodded, despite the fact that he was still in the car and there was no way the girl could see him. He checked his appearance in the rearview mirror. Skin: breakout free. Hair: unruly but still presentable. Facial hair: slight stubble. He hoped this didn't make him look like a slob. Jeremy didn't want to make a bad impression. After all, this girl was the love of his best friend's life.

He grabbed his brush from his backpack. But in

the middle of a frantic style job, Jeremy stopped. What was he so worried about, after all? Liv was *Patrick's* girlfriend, not his. This wasn't a *date*. She probably could care less about what he looked like. And, Jeremy decided, she probably didn't look too hot herself. She was too far away for him to tell, but an eight-hour road trip didn't really call for high fashion or anything.

Satisfied that he looked as good as he had to, Jeremy killed the engine. He hopped out of the car and made his way up the walk.

"Hi," Jeremy said, swallowing. "You must be Liv."

Despite the Liv hype, Jeremy was taken aback. He knew she'd be pretty—Patrick's track record was proof of that—but he had no idea she'd be so *gorgeous.*

Liv was about five-foot eight, with silky brown hair, violet-blue eyes, and an amazing body. She wore pale yellow denim shorts, a sleeveless navy blue top that tied in a knot at her waist, and a pair of brown sandals with a slight heel. A thin gold chain wrapped delicately around her ankle. *Good job, Patrick.* Wait. Who was he kidding? *Awesome job, Patrick.*

Liv smiled, nearly knocking Jeremy flat with her dazzling white teeth and dimples. "Well, actually, my name is Olivia. Only my closest friends call me Liv."

"Oh, right," Jeremy said, trying to look cool. "Well—"

Just then the mailman went by, whistling as he

7

tucked mail in the various boxes along Rosewood Lane. "Hey, Liv," he called out, his blue eyes twinkling. "Good to see you." He nodded in greeting.

"You too, Ted." Liv gave the mailman the same smile she'd just bestowed upon Jeremy, then looked back at Jeremy sheepishly.

"Just your good friends, huh?" Jeremy said, grinning.

"Sorry. I was just trying to give you a hard time." She laughed.

"Well, it's nice to finally meet you." Jeremy stuck out his hand. It seemed a bit formal, but he didn't know what else to do. "Patrick talks about you all the time."

Liv shook his hand. "I really appreciate you letting me tag along on this trip. Patrick told me how much you were looking forward to it."

Jeremy shrugged. "Yeah, well . . ." He let the rest of the sentence drift off. "You have a nice house," he offered lamely. He was always nervous when he first met people, and today was no exception.

"Thanks." Liv glanced up at the house, then ran her fingers through her hair distractedly. "It's getting kind of late, don't you think? We'd better go. Patrick's really anxious for us to get there."

By the sound of her voice, Jeremy could tell that Patrick wasn't the only anxious one. Jeremy lifted his hands in the air apologetically. "I didn't mean to be late. Traffic."

Liv nodded. "I guess everyone's trying to squeeze in the last chance at a summer vacation while they can. Well, here's my stuff." She gestured to a small mountain of bags piled on the steps. "I'm pretty sure I didn't forget anything."

"I thought I'd packed a lot," Jeremy said, surveying Liv's luggage as they carried everything to the car. He'd never seen so much stuff for just a two-week trip. There was a bright green tote bag, a regular suitcase, a garment bag, a nylon duffel bag, and some sort of purple plastic box covered with stickers of tulips and daisies. It looked like a tool kit.

"I know, I know." Liv giggled. Her laugh was light, but low. Jeremy had never heard anything like it. "I just want to be prepared," Liv explained. "I'm a little nervous about spending such a long time with the Clarks—I want to make a good impression."

"Oh, you will," Jeremy said quickly. He definitely knew Patrick would be psyched to see her. Who wouldn't? "The Clarks are great people," Jeremy said. Then he frowned. "But I don't see all this stuff going in my car. I think you'll have to leave something out."

Liv shook her head. "No, I'm sure it'll fit. We just have to be a little creative in packing," she declared firmly.

Jeremy was skeptical as he popped open the trunk. He didn't want to upset her or anything, but Liv was living in a dream world if she thought all her stuff would fit. He scratched his chin. "My trunk's not that big. I've only got the one suitcase and my backpack, but—"

Liv snapped her fingers. "Oops! I forgot—I've

9

got a present for Mr. and Mrs. Clark. I left it inside, in the hallway. Would you mind running up and getting it?" She rolled her eyes. "Then my mom can check you out in person. She wasn't too crazy about letting me drive with you, but once she spoke with Mrs. Clark about it, she decided any friend of Patrick's would be a safe chauffeur for her daughter."

"I hope the present's a small one," Jeremy said, eyeing the trunk one last time. "And if you think you can get rid of anything, do it."

"Hi, Jeremy. Nice to meet you. Veronica Carlson." Liv's mother smiled warmly, motioning him to follow her down the hall into the kitchen. Tall and slim, with sleek dark bobbed hair tucked neatly behind her ears, she looked more like an older sister than a mom. She was dressed in white cutoffs and a black form-fitting T-shirt. An older, grown-up version of Liv. *If you want to see how a girl's gonna age, check out her mom,* Jeremy recalled Mitchell saying. Things were promising for Liv, that was for sure.

The whole situation felt a little weird to Jeremy. He'd met girls' mothers before, but usually they were the mothers of someone he was dating. He'd never quite been in this situation before: not a friend, exactly, but not a date either. Kind of like a blind date without the romance. "Nice to meet you too, Mrs. Carlson."

"Please, call me Veronica," she said. She picked up a clear glass pitcher full of iced tea and lemon slices and began to stir. "Liv tells me you've driven to Pelican's Cove so many times, you know the road like the back of your hand."

"Uh, well, I, uh, guess you could say that," Jeremy stammered. *It'd be a lie, but you could say that.*

Just then Liv breezed in. Grabbing a couple bottles of chilled Evian from the refrigerator, she dumped them into an already ice-filled cooler that sat on the café-style kitchen table.

"Okay, Mom, now that you're satisfied he isn't an ax murderer, do you mind if we hit the road?" Liv said, kissing her mother lightly on the cheek.

Jeremy glanced at Liv. "No rush. I mean, I've driven this *so* many times, we'll get there plenty early." He watched Liv's cheeks flush slightly.

"Yes, well, I guess I'm just excited, that's all." Liv shot Jeremy a warning look.

Liv's mom wiped her hands on a dish towel and gave her daughter a big hug. "Have fun, honey," Veronica said. "You too, Jeremy. Wear your seat belts, and drive safely. Don't rush to get there." She kissed Liv's forehead. "My daughter is quite dear to me."

"She's pretty dear to Patrick, from what I've heard," Jeremy said, grinning. Liv looked down at the floor, the corners of her mouth turned up in a smile. "I promise I'll be careful," he added.

"Don't worry, Mom. We'll be fine. I'll call you tomorrow to let you know we're safe and sound."

Jeremy nodded. "I'll make sure she does."

Liv picked up a lavishly wrapped box that sat on the kitchen counter. "Well, I've got that present for the Clarks, so I guess we should get going now."

She gave her mom another quick kiss and motioned for Jeremy to follow her out the door.

"Why'd you tell your mom I'd been to Pelican's Cove before?" Jeremy asked as they walked out to the driveway. It was a policy of Jeremy's never to lie. He wasn't Mr. Moral or anything, but it had been his experience that once you started lying, things spun completely out of control. Maybe a teeny white lie if absolutely necessary, but lying to his friends' parents was taboo.

"Shhh!" Liv said, glancing back at the doorway, where her mother stood waving good-bye. "You have no idea what I went through. I had to fight tooth and nail just to get my mom to let me go visit Patrick at the shore. I thought if she thought you'd been there before, it'd make it easier for her to say yes." She turned her violet-blue eyes to Jeremy. "I didn't mean to make you feel like you were lying or anything," Liv said earnestly. "Really."

Jeremy couldn't blame her. If he was in love, he'd probably do the same thing. "Whatever. Now, about the luggage. I think if you take out the duffel bag, we might be able to fit all of it in, or if not, we can . . ." He trailed off. The trunk was shut. The luggage was gone. And Liv had already hopped in the car.

She smiled sweetly up out of the window at him. "See? I told you it would fit."

Amazing as it was, it was true.

They were off.

TWO

I T WAS A beautiful day for a road trip. Not that there was much of interest to see along the stretch of Pennsylvania highway they were now on—a billboard here or there, a sign advertising where to tune in during a weather emergency, the Golden Arches peeking above a curtain of Scotch pines. But it was sunny and bright.

It was still early enough for Jeremy to be psyched about the drive.

"Thirty minutes down, four hundred and fifty to go," he announced, looking at his watch.

"Thanks for that piece of uplifting information," Liv said dolefully, flicking a piece of gray carpet fuzz from her leg and taking a sip of water. "So. Is this your parents' car?" she asked, cracking open the window a few inches.

"Nope. It's all mine," Jeremy said proudly. The day he'd bought the car had been one of the best days of his life. "That's why I worked so much this summer. I'll be making payments until I'm thirty."

Liv smiled. "Well, it's nice." She took out one of the magazines she'd stuck in her tote bag and began flipping through it absently.

The two of them hadn't talked much since they pulled out of Liv's driveway. Jeremy felt a little shy. He wanted to make a good impression on Liv.

"You must be excited to see Patrick," Jeremy said after a few minutes.

"Yeah." That same upturned-corner smile from before in the kitchen lit up her face. "I am."

"Good. That's, um, good. Because I know he's really psyched to see you too." At least, Jeremy assumed he was. He'd only spoken with Patrick a couple of times since he'd left for Beach Haven at the end of June. He'd sounded really good—he'd met a lot of people, entered a local Boogie-boarding competition, gone to some parties.

Jeremy wondered how Patrick could stand to be away from Liv all summer. He didn't think he could do that if he had a serious girlfriend. He wouldn't want to let her experience a day without him. But Patrick seemed to be okay with it.

They were just different like that.

He glanced over at Liv and tried to think of something else to say. "Taking the SATs?"

Liv looked up from her magazine. "Mm-hmm. In October."

"Really? Me too," Jeremy enthused.

"Yeah, I think everybody takes them at the same time."

Duh. "Yeah. I think you're right." Jeremy chewed the inside of his lip. Very low marks on the conversation scale. Why did he feel so fidgety? So nervous and inept?

He gripped the wheel.

One thing always could make him relax. Music. Jeremy had a huge collection of CDs at home, everything from Frank Sinatra to Pearl Jam. He liked basically everything but classical, and he wasn't even opposed to that.

They didn't need to talk with the stereo on. Why hadn't he thought of that before? Slipping an old Rolling Stones tape in the tape deck, Jeremy leaned back and smiled.

There was no reason to be nervous.

This was going to be the best two weeks of the year.

The beach. Girls. His best friend. Girls. Summer. Girls. And a beautiful (sure, she was taken, but still) girl by his side, her hair flying crazily in the summer wind. All set to a terrific musical backdrop in his head.

It didn't get much better than this.

Could it possibly get any worse? Liv flipped the pages of the magazine quickly, barely bothering to read the words that danced before her eyes.

Then the song got louder. If you could even call it a song. Liv had tried to drown out the sound, the *cacophony,* but it was getting close to impossible.

Liv flipped the pages faster and faster. She began to guzzle the Evian. She'd liked Jeremy from the moment she'd met him: polite, intelligent, and nice. Not to mention cute (not that she'd noticed or anything). But that was before he began to play the steering wheel as if he were nine and it was his first drum set.

Jeremy drummed his fingers on the wheel. "Ba ba ba, ba ba ba, ba ba ba, *ba, ba!*" he sang to himself. "Yeah, yeah, uh-huh, uh-huh." His head swayed with the beat.

Liv tried to block him out. She was usually pretty good at doing that when something bugged her. Like her sister. Or her math teacher. A few minutes of drumming elapsed.

"Are you always so adept with words?" Liv asked wryly, raising her voice slightly. But Jeremy was so wrapped up in the song (which by now was blaring) that he didn't hear a word Liv said.

Back to the magazine. *Is he the right guy for you? Find out inside!* Liv chuckled to herself. It was funny how life was . . . how obvious that some people were meant to be together, while others just simply . . . weren't. She got out a pen and began circling the letters. *How does he feel about your relationship?* Liv paused. *A. He's into me—but a little gun-shy. B. My guy is definitely ready for commitment. C. Relationship? What relationship?* Definitely *B.* Liv wanted a person she could be with, share things with, a boyfriend she could

16

count on. And Patrick was all that and more.

What interests do the two of you share? A. Some—but we each have our own interests. B. Everything. We love to hang out together—we're really good friends. C. Does the X-Files *count?*

Liv chewed the end of her pen. *A? B?* To be honest, she wasn't completely sure what interested Patrick besides her. The two months they'd spent together before he left for Beach Haven had been incredible—she'd never had a serious boyfriend before, and Patrick was so attentive and loving, she never wanted it to end. And ever since they'd parted, she'd gone over every last word, last look, last thought, hungry for some new experiences to share together.

Her friend Rebecca had been a bit of a downer about the relationship. "You need to slow things down, Livvie," she'd advised.

"But he's *so* incredible," Liv had swooned.

"You think that now," Rebecca warned. "But give it time. Get to know this guy. Cute does not a relationship make."

Liv smiled to herself. Rebecca could be a pain, but she was always looking out for Liv's best interests. And she was wrong about Patrick. Liv couldn't be sure yet, of course, but he seemed like he might be The One.

She thought of the postcard he'd sent the second week he was away. On the front was a photograph of a little boy and girl, arms around each other, sitting on a beach blanket at dusk, the girl's head on the boy's shoulder. *Wish you were here . . . the beach is lonely without you. Love, Patrick.* She'd taped the postcard to her bedroom mirror, along with the photographic postcard he'd sent of himself, standing underneath a pier wearing his baggy green swim trunks, his tanned skin and bleach-blond hair making him a picture-perfect beach boy. *This guy needs one thing,* he'd written. *You!*

Definitely good boyfriend material.

Meanwhile Jeremy continued to be a one-man band in the driver's seat. Liv had swallowed her annoyance. But finally it was more than she could bear.

"You are driving me *crazy!*" she burst out, throwing her magazine on the floor. "If I hear you hum one more minute, I will yank every hair out of my head and wrap them all around your neck and pull!" Liv took a big breath. She paused. She waited for the inevitable Wild Reaction. But to her surprise, Jeremy didn't look mad. Instead he just looked shocked.

"I—I'm sorry," he said, his face reddening slightly. "I didn't mean to bug you. I just get caught up in the music and kind of tune out the world around me. Old habit." He popped the cassette out of the tape deck. "Sorry."

Liv bit her lip. She had a tendency to overreact sometimes. She didn't mean to make him feel *bad* or anything. *I mean, the guy was being pretty annoying, but he was just enjoying his music. And this is his car, after all.* She pushed the tape back into the deck. "Maybe you can just listen to it on a slightly less blaring decibel level?" she suggested meekly.

"You got it." Jeremy shifted in his seat, his eyes on the ribbon of highway in front of them.

The song was actually pretty enjoyable when it wasn't so deafening. Liv smiled. Jeremy's fingers were still tapping away on the wheel. But this time he was lip-synching.

Liv took a sip of water and looked at him thoughtfully. *Funny, he's not what I pictured him to be like.* For some reason she'd imagined Jeremy to look like Patrick. But they were complete opposites. Both guys were tall, but Jeremy was muscular, built. Patrick was leaner and more angular. Patrick had a cool, wild sort of look while Jeremy was more traditionally handsome—strong classic features, in opposition to Patrick's mischievous rebel good looks.

And there was something about Jeremy's green eyes. They looked honest. Kind.

But why am I even noticing? Liv thought guiltily.

At the beginning of the trip Liv and Jeremy had agreed to split all expenses evenly. Jeremy had felt funny at first, asking Liv to pay. Not that he was chauvinistic or anything—he was just used to paying for girls when they were with him. But going dutch would definitely be easy on his wallet. And she had been fine with the idea. In fact, she'd insisted.

"Where are you going?" Liv asked groggily.

"Gas," Jeremy answered, pointing to the sign on the roadside. It had little logos depicting several different gas stations. "Thought I'd fill up now—then hopefully we won't need to stop again." She'd fallen asleep a while ago and he'd tried to be as quiet as possible, but the change in motion had woken her up.

Jeremy pulled into the first station they came to, a Mobil. He waited expectantly for the attendant.

"You're not going to pump your own gas?" Liv asked. She sounded surprised.

Jeremy shook his head. "I hate the smell of gasoline on my hands . . . and since we're going to be driving for a while, I'd rather not stink."

Liv made a face. "But isn't full service, like, twice as expensive as self?"

"Well, it's a little more expensive, but—"

"I don't mind pumping it," Liv said. "I'd rather save the money." She began to unhook her seat belt.

Jeremy unhooked his faster. "No. There's no way I'm letting you pump our gas. I'd never hear the end of it from Patrick."

Liv smiled sweetly. "That's true." She got out of the car anyway. "Since you're going to pump, I'm going to have a look in the minimart. See if they've got anything good."

Jeremy handed her a twenty-dollar bill. "Here, pay for the gas then, will you? I'll put ten dollars worth in. And if they've got a Butterfinger or Snickers, grab me one, okay?"

Jeremy unhooked the large metal pump. He hadn't told the entire truth. True, he didn't like the smell of gas on his hands. But that was only part of it. He hated pumping his own gas because . . . he never was sure how the machine worked. Some had buttons. Some had switches. Some pumps worked right away, while others needed some coddling.

Jeremy always felt like an idiot trying to figure out how the pump worked. He was a guy, after all. He was supposed to know what to do. Instinctively.

He stood up straight. He could handle this. He took the pump off the hook, pressed Cash, and proceeded to pump with confidence. When the meter hit $10.00, he withdrew the nozzle and hung it back squarely on its hook.

Perfect.

Except for one tiny thing.

The pump's trigger stayed where it was, as if Jeremy's finger were still pulling on it. Gasoline shot out of the nozzle.

Panicked, Jeremy tried to yank the pump back off the hook, but somehow it was jammed in place, and all he ended up getting was a big splash of premium 89.

"Hey, hey, hey!" yelled the attendant who was filling up the car two aisles over.

"I can't get this thing off!" Jeremy yelled back, wrestling with the pump as if it were a boa constrictor.

Just then Liv came running out from the minimart. "Oh, my gosh," she said, trying to stifle a laugh. "You—you've got gasoline all over the place!"

Jeremy gave Liv a cold stare as the gasoline drizzled to a stop. "Really? I hadn't noticed," he said sharply. The attendant had run inside the station and returned with a huge roll of paper towels. "You're the second person that's happened to this week," he muttered, shaking his head. "We've got to get that trigger fixed." He handed Jeremy the paper towels. "You might want to go wash up inside. You stink, man!"

"Thanks for the tip," Jeremy said, stalking off to the bathroom.

"So are you hungry?" Jeremy asked. They'd been on the road for about an hour after "Pumpgate," as Liv had affectionately dubbed it. And the gasoline smell lingered.

"Not really," Liv said, taking a big bite of an apple she'd had in her tote bag. "I don't really like to stop once I'm on the road. I'd rather just get there already, you know?" She gestured to the highway as she chewed. "Besides. There aren't many places to choose from. I'd prefer not to stop at all. We'll get to Pelican's Cove much quicker if we don't."

"Hmmm. I guess if I'd had a Snickers or something back there, I wouldn't be so hungry right now," Jeremy said with a sigh. He thought longingly of the big bowl of cornflakes and rye toast he'd had for breakfast. It felt like weeks ago.

Liv bit down hard on the apple. "I told you," she said thinly. "I *was* going to get you a Snickers, but when I saw the major commotion you were causing in the gas station parking lot, I ran out to see if you were okay, and I forgot. *Sorry.*" She pursed her lips as if in thought. "I was going to get a pack of cigarettes too, but I thought it probably wasn't a good idea to be lighting up around you anytime soon. Given your condition, of course."

"Very funny," Jeremy said tersely, giving her a sidelong glance. After that comment he was *definitely* stopping for lunch, at the *first* opportunity that arose. "I didn't know you smoked."

Liv grinned mischievously. "I don't. It's a good thing too, considering that I'm driving with you."

"Ha ha."

They drove on for about ten more minutes. Then Jeremy saw what he'd been waiting for . . . what every highway traveler waits for. A giant billboard with the words Food. 2 Miles. Visions of cheeseburgers and french fries and milk shakes danced in his head.

"Food. Us. Stopping," he said, pushing his foot down hard on the accelerator.

"Um, okay," Liv said easily.

Jeremy turned to her in surprise. Okay? Man, that was easy. What had happened to *I prefer not to stop at all*? Then Jeremy noticed three empty Evian bottles lying next to Liv's tightly crossed legs.

And all was understood.

THREE

LIV STARED AT the Celica's control panel. "Am I dreaming, or didn't I just turn the air conditioner *off?*" she asked, giving the switch a hard flick to the left.

Click. Jeremy snapped the switch back to the right. "Am I dreaming, or did I just turn the air conditioner on five minutes ago?" He glanced over at Liv. Had he actually thought she'd be pleasant to travel with?

"Look, I understand you're cold. But if I don't have this thing on for at least ten more minutes, I will be a sweating pig by the time we stop for dinner." He wiped his forehead. "That is, if I'm not already."

"Too late. You are," Liv said innocently.

Jeremy grimaced. The girl was not funny.

He pretended not to notice Liv rubbing her hands back and forth, breathing on them. Out of the corner of his eye he watched as she daintily shook out a napkin (with a slight gasoline odor) and covered her feet with it.

"To retain heat," she whispered confidentially.

With a sigh Jeremy moved his hand to the control panel. *Always Mr. Nice Guy. Click.* The air conditioner was officially out of commission.

It was tough, but Jeremy managed to convince Liv that Gertie's Truck Stop Diner was as close to fine dining as they were going to manage that night.

"If it had been up to me, we would have stopped at that McDonald's twenty miles ago," Jeremy said, holding the diner's door open for Liv and several hungry-looking truckers.

Liv groaned. "Wasn't eating lunch there enough for you? Besides, I want something healthy, not fast food."

Jeremy laughed. He hated to break it to her, but Gertie's didn't exactly seem the bastion of healthy eating.

"I've got to use the ladies' room," Liv whispered. "I'll meet you at the table."

Jeremy nodded. The place was pretty full, which he hoped was a good sign. Because he was extremely hungry. Starving, actually. He noticed the truckers who'd entered behind them looking his way. Jeremy raised his eyebrows, as if to say, *What?*

The tallest one, a skinny guy in his late forties with a saggy mustache and pants to match, grinned widely. "We were just saying how pretty your girlfriend is," he said, nodding in the direction of the rest rooms. "You're one lucky guy."

Jeremy shook his head. "Uh, thanks, I guess, but she's not my girlfriend. She's just a friend. Actually she's my best friend's girlfriend."

The truckers all laughed heartily. "Best friend's girl, huh? These young guys get sneakier and sneakier," the skinny guy said to his friends.

Jeremy could feel his cheeks reddening. "No, you don't get it. It's like I said. She's—" He stopped himself just as the hostess motioned him to an empty booth. What did he care what these guys thought? He didn't have to defend his relationship with Liv to them.

Jeremy was poring over the menu when Liv rejoined him.

"Hi!" she announced brightly, sliding into the booth. She had pulled her hair up into a ponytail, and her lips had a slight sheen to them that Jeremy hadn't noticed before.

"You smell nice," Jeremy commented. "I trust it's not the rest room soap?"

"Blue Grass. By Elizabeth Arden. It's my favorite perfume," Liv said. "Just a few sprays leaves me feeling completely rejuvenated."

"Blue Grass," Jeremy repeated. He wasn't much of a perfume guy, but this was nice, natural—not too overwhelming.

"Would you like some? It might help, um, your petroleum situation," Liv said. Jeremy glared at her. She held up her hands. "Sorry, sorry. I couldn't

26

resist. But really, you don't smell anymore."

"Maybe you've just gotten used to it," Jeremy said, tossing his menu aside.

"So I guess your parents were kind of nervous about letting you go on this trip, huh?" Jeremy asked, taking a sip of his Coke as they waited for their food to arrive.

Liv shook her head. "Well, my mom was a little anxious, but my dad doesn't even know. He's in Cleveland."

Jeremy was puzzled. "On a business trip or something?"

"No." Liv fumbled with the discarded straw wrappers, folding them accordion style. "My parents are divorced. My dad moved to Cleveland a couple of years ago. I don't see him very much anymore."

Jeremy found himself reaching over and patting her hand. "That must be hard," he said sympathetically.

Liv gave a small laugh. "Yeah. Especially now that my mom has Joe around."

"Joe?"

"Her boyfriend," she said glumly.

"Oh. I take it you don't like him?"

"He's okay, I guess." Her voice quivered slightly. "It's just that I was kind of hoping my parents would get back together, you know? But it's pretty dumb, thinking like that. I mean, they got divorced when I was eleven, and I've only seen my dad, like, eight times since then." Liv unclasped her watch, then clasped it again. "Joe's not all that bad,

I guess. But I get sick of him hanging around my house, following my mom around like a lovesick puppy. He's forty, for goodness' sake!"

Jeremy tried to picture how he'd feel if his own parents were divorced and another man was seeing his mom. His mom, in one of her sweatshirts and a pair of old khakis, her curly brown hair frizzing out behind her ears and her glasses looming large on her soft, tiny face. She wasn't that bad-looking, but his mom . . . dating? He couldn't imagine it. And he didn't want to.

He said a silent prayer of thanks that his parents were married—and happily too. They'd just celebrated their twenty-first wedding anniversary in March.

"One cheeseburger deluxe, fries, and coleslaw; one chef salad with French dressing on the side," the waitress announced, balancing everything on a tray. "Lemme guess," she said to Liv. "Salad, right?"

"Right," Liv said, sliding her hand away from Jeremy's.

"Didn't mean to break up the party," the waitress said, giving Jeremy a conspiratorial wink.

Jeremy suddenly realized he had forgotten to take his hand off Liv's—he'd had it there for *minutes. Nice, Thomas.* He hoped she didn't get the wrong idea or anything.

For some reason the thought made him want to smile.

They had made excellent time after they'd left Gertie's. Right now they were somewhere between

Allentown and Philadelphia—Jeremy hadn't expected to reach this stretch of highway before 6 P.M., and it was only five-thirty.

A stretch of bumper-to-bumper, not-going-anywhere highway. They'd been stuck in traffic for what seemed like years to Jeremy. The bright red brake lights in front of them were starting to give him a headache.

Pretty soon it was six. Then it was six-fifteen. Then six-thirty.

They sat there. And sat there. And sat there. It was the worst traffic jam Jeremy had ever seen.

"It wouldn't even bother me if we were moving a little bit," Jeremy complained. "But we're just *sitting* here. I can't believe this." Up ahead people were beginning to get out of their cars. A couple of college-age guys started an impromptu game of Frisbee. An elderly couple took out some beach chairs and set up camp next to their Cadillac.

"What are these people doing?" Liv said, her voice tense. "Getting ready for a marshmallow roast? This isn't a giant picnic here. I want to get moving!" She let out an exasperated breath of air. "Who knows how long we'll be trapped!"

Jeremy unhooked his seat belt. "Stay calm. Let me go up there and see what's going on," he told her. A policeman had arrived on the scene on his motorcycle and was parked on the median. A circle of people had formed around him. "Maybe somebody can tell me something."

*　　*　　*

29

Well, that was a total waste of time, Jeremy thought as he headed back to the car.

"Well?" Liv asked hopefully as he approached.

"There's a truck overturned about six miles down the highway from here. The policeman said it might be an hour or more before they get it out of the way and traffic starts moving again." Jeremy shook his head. This really sucked. "Nothing we can do, I guess. But we've made good time already. This won't set us back much."

Liv drummed her fingers along the windowsill. It made Jeremy feel more edgy than he already did. "Where are all those people going?" she asked, pointing to a few cars that were heading off an exit ramp to the right. The sign read Spinnerstown/Trumbauersville.

"That's some kind of local exit, I guess," Jeremy said, squinting to make out the lettering. He'd never heard of those places. "I don't think it would do us any good going that way, though. I don't know where it goes."

Liv grabbed the map from the glove compartment. After studying it for a few minutes she clapped. "Okay. We're right here." Jeremy looked where she pointed. "It looks like if we take this road and follow it for about five minutes, it will take us to a bigger service road, and eventually we'll meet up with the highway again." She nibbled her pale pink fingernail. "It's a little out of our way, sure, but since we're stuck here for who knows how long, I think it's our best bet."

"Let *me* see the map," Jeremy asked, leaning over. A wave of Blue Grass washed over him.

"Why? Don't you trust me?" Liv asked, holding the map up to her chest. "I'm an expert map reader."

Jeremy laughed. "I just don't want to get us lost. Patrick would kill me if anything happened to you."

It was Liv's turn to laugh. "Nothing's going to happen. Look, I listened to you for dinner," Liv countered. "Now you listen to me. And besides, where's your sense of adventure?"

"Okay, okay. You've convinced me." Jeremy looked over his shoulder to make sure the coast was clear and drove the car onto the shoulder. "Trumbauersville, here we come."

"I thought you said you knew where this would take us," Liv complained, staring out the window. "We're in the boondocks!" They had been driving for more than twenty minutes now along winding, hilly roads, amidst heavy Pennsylvania foliage. There were no route signs. None. Nothing that could give them any clue as to where they were.

Jeremy could feel his blood growing warm. "Wait a minute here, Liv. Weren't *you* the one who said you were an expert map reader? Have you forgotten whose idea it was to get off the highway? I had the route all planned."

"Then you should have stayed with it," Liv said petulantly. She stuck out her tongue at him.

Now his blood was starting to boil. He forced himself to count to ten. "C'mon," he said finally.

31

"Where's your sense of adventure?"

"I left it back there ten miles ago." She breathed in deeply. "Now look where you've gotten us."

"Look, Liv. If you weren't so hot and bothered to get to Pelican's Cove, I would never have attempted this lame plan," Jeremy said defensively.

Liv crossed her arms and stared straight ahead. The road seemed to twist and turn for endless miles. Other than one or two passing cars, they had the road to themselves. Ahead of them the sun was just starting to set, a brilliant burst of red and orange visible through the thick, heavy forest branches.

Jeremy sighed. It was crazy to argue. He didn't want to be driving around on roads he didn't know any more than she did. He couldn't wait to get to Patrick's. He felt like he'd been in the car for days. Long days.

"Sunsets this time of year are nice, huh?" Jeremy remarked, ignoring Liv's silence. "It's like after summer has given us the best it's got, it whips out some awesome sunsets it's saved in reserve as an end-of-the-season bonus or something."

Liv gave him a reluctant smile. "Yeah."

Jeremy glanced over at her. So what if getting off the highway was a bad idea? They had plenty of gas. They still had made good time. And despite their petty arguments he *had* been enjoying her company.

"Liv?"

"What?"

"Let's not argue. Who cares how we got here?" Jeremy said reasonably. "We both want to get to Pelican's Cove as soon as possible, right? Patrick's not going anywhere. He'll be there."

Liv seemed to relax a bit, her arms unfolding. She didn't say anything. But at least she didn't look as tense as she had, Jeremy noticed with relief.

After a few more minutes of driving Liv picked up the map.

"Maybe you'd better pull over. It's getting kind of dark. I think we should turn around or something," she suggested. "I goofed up."

After poring over the map for several moments Jeremy realized their mistake. Apparently they had mistook a fork in the road as a right turn and so missed the right turn they were supposed to make after the fork. It had looked so easy when he'd studied the map before.

"Pretty simple, really," Liv said slowly, trailing her pen along the map. "We're here." She made a little blue *X*. "If we turn around and go back about ten miles, we should come to where we missed the turn."

"We make the turn, and in about ten minutes we'll be back on the highway," Jeremy finished. For a moment there he'd started to think they'd never get out of this forest.

"Exactly," said Liv, making another *X* where the highway was. "Time to connect the *X*s." She smiled one of her megawatt smiles. "Onward, Chauffeur Thomas."

Jeremy made a U-turn and headed back in the

direction they'd just come. The last minutes of daytime were disappearing, and Jeremy was glad to be heading back to the highway, back to more familiar territory.

Liv peered into the woods, trying to make out landmarks in the fading dusk. "Yes, yes—okay. I remember passing that big rock over there before. I think we just have to go a few more miles, then—" Jeremy heard a gasp. "Hey! Watch out!"

"Huh? Oh, jeez," Jeremy muttered, swerving the car sharply to the right. A fat raccoon with big, dark eyes appeared out of nowhere. It ran right in front of the car. Jeremy gripped the wheel and braced himself.

Smack.

Jeremy's head snapped back at the force of the impact. He realized his foot was pushing down hard on the brake, and instinctively he pushed down even harder, bracing himself for the sound of crunching metal.

But except for the slight jingle of the keys in the ignition, it was totally quiet. Jeremy shifted the car into park and steadied his shaking hands. "Are you okay?" he asked, turning to Liv. Her face was ashen.

Liv nodded and let go of the door handle she had been clutching. "I think so."

"Good. I'm fine, you're fine, that stupid raccoon is fine. Everything is fine. Except the car."

Sure, Jeremy had avoided hitting the raccoon. But instead he'd managed to ram the front of the Celica into a decayed old tree stump, conveniently positioned in front of his right tire. Already it was flat. A large flap of rubber lay torn off on the ground, and the last sighs of air escaping mingled with the sounds of the forest, chirping and humming and clicking.

"At least we didn't hit the raccoon," Liv pointed out.

"Whoopee," Jeremy said under his breath. What lousy luck.

He slammed the door and crouched down to get a good look. At least there wasn't any major damage to the car itself. He could see a few tiny scratches along the front bumper. That wasn't too bad. He could hide them with some paint pretty easily. And he had the spare tire, the "doughnut," in the back. Changing a tire in the middle of nowhere wasn't going to be a picnic, but things could be worse.

He stood up and stretched. Then he reached inside the car window and pushed the trunk button.

"This shouldn't take too long," he called to Liv over the hatch. "But if you wouldn't mind, maybe you could get out the owner's manual from the glove compartment? I think it runs through how to change a tire." He began hauling out Liv's luggage from the trunk.

"Jeremy?" He jumped, startled to feel Liv's cool hand on his arm. She looked as if she was about to cry.

"Hey, don't worry," he said, smiling gently. A few strands of hair had fallen loose from her ponytail. It made her look soft and sweet. Man, she was pretty. "I've changed a tire before," he said, glad to reassure her. "Really, it's no big deal. Just read the instructions to me so I don't forget something major. We'll be on the road again in no time." He carefully placed Liv's garment bag on the ground and picked up her duffel.

Liv shook her head. "No, you don't understand," she said nervously, biting her lip. "About that spare tire in the trunk? See, the reason I was able to fit in all my luggage . . ."

FOUR

THERE WERE NO good Samaritans left in the world.

Or maybe there were just no drivers left in the world. Because in the thirty minutes Jeremy and Liv had spent yelling, crying, and generally feeling hopeless, not one single car had passed them. Nada. Not a car, not a minivan, not a motorcycle—heck, not even an Amish horse and buggy.

Jeremy stared hard at the trunk. It was as if he looked long and hard enough, the doughnut would miraculously appear, attach itself to the wheel rim, and they could be on their way.

He couldn't *believe* Liv had done such a stupid thing. Sure, guys did stupid things—and he was the first to admit he'd done plenty. But taking out the spare tire just before you hop in the car for an eight-hour road trip? Nope. Guys might be clueless, but you'd never meet one who'd pull an idiot move like that.

"Okay, okay," Liv said, continuing to pace around the car for about the hundredth time now. "We've got to think logically and do something." She stopped to peer down at the torn tire. "Are you sure that you can't drive it like it is? Maybe there's a gas station nearby. Maybe you'd only have to drive it five more miles or something."

Jeremy gave her a sidelong glance. "I thought you said you were going to think *logically*," he said tersely. "There's no way I can drive on that. It'd be like driving on the rim." He leaned against the doorframe. "Our only chance of getting to the Clarks' tonight is if someone stops to pick us up." He looked around. "And that's not looking very promising at the moment."

Liv sat down on the hood—and leaped up as if she'd been shocked.

"Ow!" she exclaimed, rubbing the backs of her bare legs.

Jeremy winced. "The engine got hot from the drive. You better watch yourself."

"Great," Liv mumbled. "Leg burn and a flat tire. What more could go wrong?" She stepped down purposefully on a large branch that lay on the side of the road. It made a sharp *crack*. "Patrick is going to be freaking out if we don't get there soon," Liv said suddenly. Her voice trembled slightly. "He really is." She wrapped her arms around herself.

"Yeah, I know." Jeremy tapped his fingers along the Celica's roof. He'd been racking his brain for the past half hour, trying to come up with a solution. "But what do you want me to do?"

"I want you to get us out of here!" Liv burst out. "I'm tired and I'm hungry and I'm cold. And I don't want to be out here in the woods! I want to be at Pelican's Cove. With Patrick." Frustrated, she gave the flat tire a hard kick.

"That's really going to help things," Jeremy said dryly. "Uh, did you forget why we're in this situation in the first place? If Miss I've-got-to-bring-my entire-wardrobe had left a few fashion accessories at home, we'd be driving this very moment."

Liv sniffled. "Make me feel even worse than I do, why don't you?" She sighed. "I know it's my fault. I'm sorry."

Jeremy shook his head. "We're both just frustrated. It doesn't do any good to point fingers." The cool Pennsylvania air made him shiver. "Maybe we'd better get back in the car. It's getting kind of cold out here." He hated to point out the obvious, but it was apparent that this was not a very popular road. And he wasn't too keen on flagging down help at this point anyway. He felt more out of control in the dark, more at someone else's mercy. Better to spend the night in the car, catch some z's, and get help in the morning.

Liv bit her lip. "So I guess we're really giving up on going anywhere tonight," she said, swallowing.

Jeremy smiled halfheartedly. "You know I want to see Patrick just as much as you do," he told her gently. "But you can see that we're pretty much out of luck right now." He patted her shoulder. "You wait. Tomorrow we'll wake up early, and if no one drives by, we'll start walking. Someone's bound to help us."

"I guess you're right," Liv answered resignedly. "So. What side of the car do you normally sleep on?"

It was pretty noisy at first, considering they were in the middle of the woods and it was after nine o'clock. Jeremy was surprised at all the action taking place. Crickets chirped. Cicadas hummed. The leaves blew softly in the barely perceptible wind— but the sheer volume of leaves made a little noise sound like a lot. And every now and then a sharp *crack* would reach his ears.

At first he and Liv exchanged uneasy glances. But then Jeremy began to relax. After all, they were safely ensconced in the car. And, Jeremy pointed out, he had The Club. Anybody who wanted to mess with them would have to deal with a whack of The Club first.

"How safe do you think we are out here?" Liv asked apprehensively. She was dwarfed in Jeremy's oversize navy blue Penn State sweatshirt. "Guaranteed to make you sweat in about one hour," he'd said when he got it out of the trunk for her, along with an old tartan blanket he'd kept in the car since his last picnic. "Like, do you think there are lots of wild animals around us?" Liv continued. She framed her face with her hands and stared out into the darkness. "I can't see anything. The window's getting all steamy."

"There probably are bears around here," Jeremy

said thoughtfully. "They can smell food for miles away. They don't really mean to attack people, but if they think they're being threatened or you interrupt them when they're hunting for food, it can be deadly. It depends on the kind of bear—grizzly, brown . . ."

Liv nodded. "My aunt and uncle went camping on the Delaware Water Gap once, and they left a big cooler near the picnic area when they went to sleep. My uncle wanted to put it in their van, but my aunt said not to bother."

"Bad move," Jeremy interjected.

"You can say that again," Liv agreed. "Later that night a bear came into their campsite, grabbed the cooler, and threw it again and again onto the picnic tables until it burst open and all the food spilled out." She laughed. "Boy, did that bear have a feast."

"Was anyone hurt?" Jeremy asked.

"No, but my aunt and uncle were famished. They finally got food at some nearby convenience store. My uncle kept the top of the cooler—it has huge holes in it made from the bear's claws. They've got it hanging up in their garage."

"Cool camping souvenir," Jeremy said.

"Mmmm."

Jeremy tilted his seat back. From his vantage point he could see a sliver of the sky—it was peppered with twinkling, sparkling stars. His lower back ached slightly—it always did when he'd been riding in a car for a long time.

"This is so ironic," Liv said after a while.

41

"What is?" Jeremy asked.

Liv swept her arm in front of her. "This. Me. You. Me in a car, spending the night with a guy that I just met." She giggled. "My mom will flip when she hears this."

"Really?" Jeremy said. "She seemed pretty cool."

Liv looked over at him. "Yeah. My mom is cool." She raised her eyebrows. "But I still don't think she'd be too keen about this."

"Too bad you weren't stuck here with Patrick instead of me," Jeremy commented. "I mean, it could be kind of romantic if you were stranded somewhere with your boyfriend or girlfriend, or at least someone you were interested in. . . ." He trailed off. *What am I talking about? I sound like a total idiot.* Jeremy stared out the window. *Like she doesn't realize what I'm saying is that if you're stuck in the car with a member of the opposite sex that you find attractive, certain things can happen. Good things.*

Liv pulled the seat-adjustment lever and pushed her seat back to meet Jeremy's. "I guess so," she said, yawning. "Anyplace can be romantic if you want it to be." She gave Jeremy a tired little smile. "Really, I am sorry about this. I know it was my fault, and I feel bad you have to be stuck here with me."

Jeremy started to say that that wasn't what he meant at all. And he wouldn't use the word *stuck*. In fact, he was kind of enjoying the whole situation.

But it was no use.

Liv had fallen asleep.

FIVE

SHE WRAPPED HER arms seductively around his neck. "Oh, Jeremy. I've waited so long for this." Softly Liv began to nuzzle his cheek, his ear, his hair.

Jeremy held her tightly, feeling her heart pounding through the soft white satin blouse she wore. "I didn't know you felt this way about me," he whispered, kissing her forehead. "And you smell so good. Is it Blue Grass?"

Liv nodded. "Yes," she purred, leaning against him. "You're so brilliant, Jeremy. I love the way you stocked the cereal boxes. All color coded and everything."

"You're so beautiful, Liv." His hands smoothed her hair back from her perfect face. "I knew you'd notice."

Liv's lips curved into an alluring smile. "I love you, Jeremy. Just you, Jeremy. Jeremy. Jeremy . . ."

"Jeremy!"

He sat up like he'd been branded with a hot iron. "What!"

Liv clapped a hand over his mouth. "Shhh!" She pointed out the front window. "Look!"

Still half asleep, Jeremy gazed out the front window. Standing in front of the car were a giant buck and a smaller doe, illuminated in a shaft of moonlight. The buck's body was huge and powerful looking, his antlers firm and majestic. The doe was smaller and more gentle looking. They weren't too close, about three feet away—but close enough for Jeremy to see the soft, short brown hairs that covered their bodies and the wet early morning dew that dampened their hooves.

The buck's giant front hoof pawed through the layer of leaves and dirt, moving in a small circle. The doe stood close by his side, her hoof moving too but not as much. When the buck found something to eat, he rubbed against the doe, as if to say, *I'll wait for you to eat.*

Liv let out a small gasp. "He's letting her go first."

Jeremy nodded in the semidarkness, still reeling from the dream he'd been in a few moments before. "I just can't believe how big they are."

After foraging for a few more minutes the deer moved down to the small stream. Their heads bent in unison as they drank.

"I wish we could get a picture of this," Liv whispered. "They're so beautiful." She reached down slowly, trying not to startle the deer with her movement. "I think my camera's in my tote bag—"

"It wouldn't come out, I don't think," Jeremy whispered back. "It's too dark. And the flash would probably—"

Suddenly the deer looked straight at the car, meeting Jeremy and Liv's shocked gaze. After several seconds they turned and fled into the night.

It was as if they'd never been there at all.

"Wow." Jeremy shook his head. "That was pretty cool."

"It was like they were trying to tell us something!" Liv said excitedly. "Did you see the way they looked at us? They looked so peaceful."

After seeing the deer, falling asleep was impossible. Jeremy was too wound up. He could tell Liv felt the same way.

"They were just so awesome," said Liv.

"They were," Jeremy agreed. "See? Spending the night out here has its advantages."

Liv smiled. "This might sound crazy, but seeing them looking for food made me realize that I'm starving!"

"Welcome to the club," Jeremy said with mock cheerfulness. "My stomach's been rumbling for the past hour and a half."

He rummaged through the paper bags that littered the backseat. The food inventory was not the greatest: leftover McDonald's apple pie, several soggy french fries, a brown-spotted, smushed-in banana, an ice-diluted cup of Coke, and half a bottle of warm Evian.

"So you never told me where you want to go to school," Liv said, giving a droopy french fry a critical once-over.

Jeremy tossed an empty cassette case back into the holder. "Probably Penn State. My brother goes there, but it's so huge that it's not like I'd ever see him. Most of their programs are pretty good." Jeremy was still undecided on a major. Something in the liberal arts. What, he didn't know. He'd been thinking lately about becoming a teacher. He liked kids, and the idea of making a difference in the world, hackneyed as it might be, appealed to him.

"What's bad about seeing your brother? Don't you get along?" Liv inquired.

Jeremy chuckled, taking a sip of the Coke. "No, it's not that. Sometimes you just want to be on your own. He really digs the big brother role, and while I love him, I don't need him to run my life."

Liv attempted to curl up on her side. "Believe me, I understand. My older sister, Andrea, is a total pain in the butt. She's always giving me advice that I don't need," Liv said exasperatedly. "But she's the lucky one this summer. She's trekking through Europe right now with her French boyfriend, Jean-Paul."

Jeremy whistled. "Ooo-la-la. Sounds *très romantique.*"

"You speak French?" Liv asked in surprise.

"Sort of. I had to take it to fill the language requirement at Millcreek." Jeremy shrugged. "But I have to say, I kind of like it. Our French club went on a trip to Montreal this past spring. It was pretty cool hearing everybody speak French. And the food was pretty good too. Crepes and stuff."

"I've studied French for four years," Liv said. "I really love it." She closed her eyes. "My dream is to visit Paris someday and go to the top of the Eiffel Tower at night, with all the lights of the city flashing up on me. I'd eat chocolate croissants every day, buy really cool French clothes, and wear big, mysterious sunglasses and a chiffon scarf around my head."

Jeremy laughed. "So does that mean you're going to study abroad in the City of Lights?" he asked.

Liv rolled her eyes. "No. *That* was my fantasy. My reality is probably Penn State, like you. Or maybe somewhere in Ohio, like Miami of Ohio or the University of Dayton," Liv said, ticking them off on her fingers. "I've been planning on studying pharmacy, but I've changed my mind." She paused. "I'm going to do what I've wanted to do, really, but have been too chicken to say it."

"Don't keep me in suspense."

"Veterinary science. I'd like to be a vet," Liv said matter-of-factly. "There. I said it." She grinned. "I love animals. And I've always done well in science," she added proudly.

"That's great," Jeremy said admiringly. "I can see you as a vet."

"Really?" Liv asked, flushing.

"Sure. Why not?" Jeremy answered. "You're smart, caring, tender—just what all those sick puppies out there need. I bet you'd make an awesome vet."

Liv smiled. "Well, thanks."

It was amazing. They'd driven for seven hours with nothing to say. But suddenly the words came easily. Jeremy couldn't believe how much they had in common. They both liked to ice-skate—but no more than one hour at a time. They loved rainy days in the spring and the zoo in the summer. They each had older siblings who drove them nuts. They liked the same movies—especially action films. Liv's mom bought her groceries at the store where Jeremy worked. And they both loved to hang out at the Erie Art Museum.

"Favorite food?" Liv asked.

"Pizza."

Liv nodded, taking a sip of water. "Correct. Color?"

"Green."

"The answer is purple. But I'll let that one slip. Favorite class?"

"Study hall." They both laughed in unison.

It was wild. He'd never spent so much time with a girl without a break—but he didn't want one. There was so much to learn about her.

"This is something, huh?" Jeremy said. He couldn't believe he'd met a girl who liked so many of the same things he did. He'd never met anybody like her.

"Yeah." Liv took a sip of the Evian.

Jeremy studied her face for a moment. A drop of water lay on Liv's lower lip. She didn't seem to feel it. "Here," Jeremy said softly, leaning over. He reached up and gently brushed the droplet away . . . but his fingers lingered. Jeremy moved his finger along Liv's bottom lip. Then his body moved closer to hers.

Suddenly they were kissing.

Liv's lips were soft and moist. Jeremy could feel the heat radiating from them. Tenderly he grazed her lips. He kissed her teasingly, playfully. Liv teased back. The kiss grew more and more intense. Jeremy's hands reached up and loosened her ponytail. A soft cascade of hair spilled out onto his fingers.

"Liv," he murmured, his hand moving down her back, pressing her even closer.

Without warning, Liv pulled away sharply. Her eyes were huge and wild.

"W-What are you doing?" She gasped, wiping the back of her hand roughly against her mouth.

Jeremy licked his lips. "I—I . . . ," he stammered helplessly. "I don't know, I didn't mean to, I—"

"Don't you ever do that again!" Liv said, her voice shaking. She pulled the blanket that was covering her legs up tightly to her face. "What's wrong with you?" Then she turned her back on him.

Jeremy's heart was pounding with fear and with passion. Did he imagine it, or didn't she want to kiss him just as much as he wanted to kiss her? His hands shook slightly as he smoothed back his hair. What had he done?

A kiss like that couldn't be one-sided. It was too powerful. Too incredible. Too intense.

Too real.

Jeremy stared at Liv's back. She was coiled up as far away from him as possible.

She's Patrick's girlfriend. What have I done? he thought, his heart and his brain slamming into each other like some crazy dancers in a mosh pit.

The full force of what happened hit him.

It wasn't that he had just kissed his best friend's girlfriend. It was far worse—Jeremy had fallen for the one girl he couldn't have.

SIX

THE NEXT MORNING dawned clear and bright, the sun making its way up through the forest leaves to the sky high above.

Jeremy glanced at the dashboard clock. 7:10 a.m. He yawned. His whole body ached, especially his neck, which had been twisted sideways on the headrest all night long. He'd had a restless, uneven night, tossing and turning on the small, hard seat. It had taken him forever to fall asleep, but sometime after 5 A.M. he'd zonked out.

Jeremy stretched his arms and looked over at Liv. Or more precisely, Liv's empty seat. She was gone. Jeremy's eyes darted into the backseat and then zeroed in on her door, slightly ajar.

She wouldn't have done anything stupid, like trying to walk for help by herself, would she? The events of the night before came rushing into his head, flooding his brain. He couldn't believe he'd done what he did—that *they* had done what they did.

This isn't any girl, Jeremy. It's Patrick's girl-friend. Patrick's. Girlfriend. The words rolled through his mind like a never-ending movie trailer. He pictured the guys at school standing around with their jaws open. *You did what, Thomas?* Jeremy felt sick at the thought of what happened. *And now she's disappeared.*

She probably wanted nothing to do with him, Jeremy realized miserably. He got out of the car and shook out his arms and legs. "Liv?" he called. His voice echoed through the early morning air. "Yo, Liv?"

He listened carefully and soon heard the sound of branches crackling.

"Can't a person have some privacy?" Liv muttered as she came trudging through the trees. Jeremy thought Liv looked even prettier in the morning than she had last night. And she'd looked pretty good then too. Her eyes were puffy and sleepy looking, and her cheeks had a pale pink hue. She'd put her hair back up in a ponytail.

"Sorry," Jeremy said, flustered. Come to think of it, he had to go to the bathroom too. "I'll be back," he called out, making a path through the woods.

When he returned, Liv was crouched down in front of the car. "You can see the deer tracks here," she said, pointing to the ground.

Jeremy nodded. "That was pretty cool last night," he said. He felt his face turning red. "The deer, I mean." Before he could further embarrass himself, he heard a noise in the distance. Either he was imagining things or there was some kind of vehicle coming toward them from down the highway.

Liv leaped up. "Someone's coming."

Jeremy followed Liv as she ran out to the road and flagged down a forest green minivan as it came over the crest of the hill.

The twenty-something driver came to a stop and rolled down his window. "You guys stuck?" A woman wearing a flowered dress sat beside him, and a tiny baby slept peacefully in a car seat in the back.

"Yeah. We've got a flat tire and no spare," Jeremy told him.

"Can you help us?" Liv blurted out. "We're totally desperate."

The man turned to the woman, who Jeremy guessed was his wife. She shook her head slightly. "We're on our way to a family reunion," she said apologetically, leaning over her husband. "We'll be late if we stay." She grinned. "And this is the first time my parents are going to see Benjamin. We can't keep them waiting."

Her husband eyed the Celica. "There's an autobody shop about ten miles down the road. We'll stop and send someone back to help you," he offered. "Okay?"

"Okay," Jeremy said, shoving his hands in his pockets and stepping back from the window. "Thanks." He waved as the couple pulled away.

"How could you just let them go like that?" Liv exploded, stomping her foot. "Our first chance at salvation and you let our rescuers get away!"

Jeremy sighed. He could understand her frustration, but she was being a little ridiculous. "Let's get back to reality here, Liv. Other than holding them hostage, I didn't see many alternatives to 'no.'"

Liv dropped down along the roadside. "They'd better send help," she mumbled, her eyes narrowing into little slits.

Jeremy shivered with mock fear. "They'd *better*."

Liv glared at him.

Twenty minutes later a tow truck with the words Sal's Autobody printed on its side pulled up.

"Anybody here need a tow?" said the tall black-haired guy looking out the window.

"We do," Liv said, grabbing her tote bag and hopping into the cab of the truck. "How fast can you change a tire?"

Jeremy eyed the box of doughnuts on the counter.

"Here, help yourself," said Sal, gesturing toward the carton. "You guys must be starved."

"Thanks," Jeremy said gratefully, picking the biggest one in the box. "I wish we'd had a *doughnut* last night, don't you, Liv?"

She scowled as she cradled the phone next to her ear. Liv had wanted to call the Clarks to let them know they were okay as soon as they arrived at the shop. "The line is busy!" she said in frustration, slamming down the receiver. "Who could they be talking to at this hour?"

"They're probably trying to find out if we're okay," Jeremy remarked. He knew the Clarks were probably frantic by now. He hoped that they hadn't called his parents. His mother would be in tears, his father pacing back and forth, Mitchell worried but still smug and self-serving—all for a flat tire.

Jeremy dialed his own number. After four rings: "Hello. You've reached the Thomas residence. Leave your name and number, and we'll call you back as soon as possible. Thank you." Jeremy frowned. Where could his parents be at eight-thirty Sunday morning? It was too early for church. Then he remembered. They were going sailing with their friends the Johnsons on Lake Erie. They liked to go out early and watch the sun rise, over muffins and coffee.

"Uh, hi, it's me," Jeremy said to the machine. "I just wanted to let you know in case you were worried that everything's fine. We kind of got stuck in the woods last night, but we're okay, and we'll be at the Clarks soon in case they call you. Okay? Don't worry. Love you. Bye." He hung up, hoping his message didn't sound too mushy.

"They weren't home?" Liv moaned.

"Nah, they're out on the lake. But we'll be at Patrick's soon anyway. No use worrying about it now."

Liv insisted on paying for half of the bill. "You don't need to do that," Jeremy told her, pushing her fistful of money away.

"I want everything to be fair and square," Liv said staunchly, pushing the money back. "There's no need for you to pay for something that was my fault in the first place."

"Well, if you insist . . ." Jeremy trailed off.

"I do." Liv snapped her wallet shut. "I hate feeling like I owe people things."

"It's official then, Liv," Jeremy said, handing the money to Sal and signing the bill he'd stuck in front of him. "You don't owe me anything."

And as he signed his name he couldn't help but notice that Liv's upper lip quivered slightly as he said the words.

The silence in the car was deafening.

"It feels good to be moving again," Jeremy said, his voice sounding falsely cheerful to Liv's ears. They'd retraced the path they'd taken the night before and located the spot where they'd missed the turn. Now they were on the highway again.

"Yeah. It does," Liv said brightly, pushing the window button down to get some fresh air. She was trying to act normal, as if everything was completely okay between the two of them. But it wasn't. All she could think of was the way Jeremy had looked at her last night. How his lips had felt against hers.

Liv hadn't had many kisses like that before. In fact, she'd never had a kiss like that before.

It held promise.

And it felt real.

Liv had kissed four guys in her life. There was Tom Williams, her first kiss. That had been a little awkward, but on the whole it was a pretty good kiss. They'd gone out for a couple months during freshman year, but it was pretty innocent stuff: hanging out at basketball games, sitting together in the library, going out for pizza in a big group. Then along came cute Ashley Lauder, and Liv was history.

Brett Shueman was Liv's next boyfriend. They dated on and off during her sophomore year. Brett was nice (and a much more experienced kisser than Tom), but he was definitely too wrapped up in football to handle a serious relationship. And that was fine with Liv, who managed to break up with him and still be on good terms. Right before she met Patrick, Liv had been out twice with Ray Butler. But they just weren't getting along all that well.

And then she met Patrick.

When Patrick came into her life, Liv realized that she'd never taken guys seriously before. She'd never had a boyfriend like Patrick. He bought her roses. And not just red ones, like everyone else got from their boyfriends. Patrick liked peach-colored roses. He said they were unique, just like her. Patrick would call unexpectedly, just to say he was thinking about her. He'd even dedicated a song to her on *Night Vibes,* the radio call-in program. Patrick was different. Special. Liv's friends couldn't wait to hear what romantic thing he did next.

Liv's thoughts drifted to Jeremy. He'd been silent for the past half hour now. *The way he said my name. Liv. Slowly. Meaningfully.* No one had ever pronounced her name that way. Not even

Patrick. She was embarrassed to admit it, but that morning she'd whispered her name the way Jeremy had, lingering over the *v*. Luckily no one except the birds had heard her.

Liv snuck a glance at Jeremy's profile. He looked tired, but other than that, Jeremy looked just as hunklike as he did yesterday. Same clear green eyes, same strong Roman nose, same soft red lips.

Jeremy's lips . . . the pit in Liv's stomach began to ache. She didn't like herself or what she was thinking. Did she need to remind herself that she was in a relationship? A committed relationship with Patrick Clark, someone she cared about deeply? Fooling around with his best friend was not something she'd ever imagined herself doing. She wasn't that kind of girl. She had morals. Standards.

And cheating on her boyfriend was something she was completely, totally against.

"Do you mind if I turn on the radio?" Jeremy asked, jarring Liv from her reverie of boyfriends of summers past and present.

"Go ahead," Liv said, thankful to have some noise in the car. Jeremy pushed the button and a twangy country-western tune blared from the speakers. Liv toyed with the dial for a few moments, but all she could find was either country western or Sunday morning evangelical programs. Neither was very satisfying.

The minutes passed slowly. "Hungry?" Jeremy asked. He seemed to be searching for something to say.

She'd been starving last night, but thinking about

Patrick and what she had risked by kissing Jeremy had made her lose her appetite. "Well, if you see a Burger King or something, I wouldn't mind stopping for a quick cup of coffee." *A wake-up back to reality,* she thought sternly. *Make that a double espresso.*

Jeremy nodded. "There should be one up ahead."

The silence in the car grew even louder.

Finally Liv couldn't stand it any longer. "Look," she said, trying to choose her words carefully. "What happened last night between us, well, um—" She looked down at the floor. "It was a mistake. A *big* mistake." Liv waited for Jeremy to say something, but his lips were pressed tightly together, his eyes focused straight ahead.

She continued. "I just didn't want you to get the wrong impression of me. I—I'm not the kind of girl who cheats on her boyfriend. I've never done that sort of thing, and I'm not about to. I just wanted you to know that."

Jeremy shot her a pointed look. "If you think I'm in the habit of kissing my best friend's girlfriends, let me assure you that *I'm* not that kind of guy."

Liv's hands were moist and sweaty, and she wiped them nervously on her legs. "No. I'm sure you aren't. I wasn't trying to accuse you of anything. I—"

"Let's get one thing straight here," Jeremy said in a low voice. "You were angry at me last night, and I understand why. It was wrong of me to kiss you like that. But you—you kissed me too, Liv." He paused. "Didn't you?"

Liv buried her face in her hands. She couldn't believe that they were actually having this conversation. It was totally mortifying. "I just want to forget about this whole thing, okay?" she said wearily. "You were tired, I was tired. Things . . . happen. We weren't in a clear frame of mind." She looked over at Jeremy. "Can you just promise me not to mention this again? Ever?" she whispered desperately.

Jeremy clutched the wheel. "I see," he said at last. "You're afraid I'm going to tell Patrick." He shook his head. "Are you crazy? Patrick's like a brother to me. I'd never hurt him." They drove in silence for a while. Liv stared out the window as they whipped by an endless stream of trees and fast-food billboards. She felt embarrassed and angry. How could she have done something so stupid? Something that could jeopardize her relationship with Patrick?

"Liv?" Jeremy looked over at her. "If this is how you want it, then fine. What happened last night was a big mistake between you and me. And as far as I'm concerned, it never happened."

Liv tried to swallow the huge lump that had formed in her throat. "Thank you." The words sounded small and thin.

"No problem," Jeremy answered, his voice clipped.

Liv willed herself to think positively. After all, she was going to be spending two fun-filled weeks at the Jersey shore with Patrick. She'd be staying in a gorgeous house, surrounded by nice people and doing lots of fun things. Everything was going to be great. She and Patrick would get along fantastically.

Last night with Jeremy would be forgotten, and they'd all have the summer of their lives.

Liv glanced up just as the Celica sped by a road sign. Jersey Shore. 45 Miles.

Nothing's changed, Liv told herself. *I'm still Patrick Clark's girlfriend and we have a great relationship.* But if everything was so great, why did she feel so miserable?

SEVEN

Jeremy ran his tongue over his front teeth, which felt slimy and bumpy all at once. "Do you have any of those breath mints left?"

He reached for the curlicue roll of mints Liv dangled in front of him.

"Not so fast. There's just one left. And I hate to share." Liv pulled the mints out of his reach.

"Your choice. But if you don't give it up, you'll have to live with my dog breath until we get there." Jeremy opened his mouth. "Hahhhhh." He breathed out deeply.

"It's yours," Liv said immediately, handing it over.

Jeremy sighed as he turned the car onto Ocean Parkway. "Not that you'd have to suffer that long anyway. We're almost there."

We're almost there. . . .

To get to the summer community of Beach

Haven, you followed a series of local roads from the New Jersey Turnpike about twenty miles to a bridge that crossed a waterway and brought you out onto the main drag of Ocean Parkway. The Clarks' house was tucked away down one of the tangle of sandy side roads that snaked off toward the beach.

The oceanfront house was huge, more like a mansion than a summer cottage. Sided with weather-beaten cedar shingles turned gray from years of sea spray and wind, it sat back from the main road, hidden and protected by a tall picket fence. A colorful sailboat banner snapped sharply atop a white metal flagpole. A two-car garage sat at the right of the gravel driveway entrance, and a small paved basketball court was off to the garage's left. A carved wooden pelican stood as a sentry at the gate, a tiny sign hanging at its side. It read Pelican's Cove.

Jeremy slowly drove the car through the gate and came to a stop next to the Clark's Camry.

"At last," Liv said, staring up at the house. Jeremy watched as she dabbed her lips with some stuff from a tiny pot. She seemed really anxious to get inside. She ran her hairbrush hurriedly through her hair. "I can't believe we're finally here," she bubbled.

Jeremy nodded halfheartedly. The initial excitement of the visit had waned for him. If Patrick discovered what had happened between him and Liv, he'd never forgive Jeremy. And Jeremy wouldn't blame him. *He would totally kill me.* He and Patrick could read each other so well. . . . After

63

their eight years of friendship, there was nothing they didn't tell each other.

But this . . .

Jeremy couldn't deny the way he felt. It sounded ridiculous, but in the twenty-four hours he'd spent with Liv, Jeremy had been blown away by his intense feelings. Despite what he'd told her, Jeremy knew he wasn't just messing around in a moment of passion. It was more than that. A lot more. And Jeremy didn't know what to do. *I mean, here I am having kissed Patrick's girlfriend, and even though I feel majorly guilty, all I can do is wonder if it will happen again.*

Jeremy hadn't been able to bring it up all morning. Now, when he felt like he might have the courage to talk, they were driving down the road to the house. They had gotten here too soon. Jeremy groaned inwardly. Couldn't he have gotten them lost? Taken another detour? He didn't want to face Patrick just yet. He couldn't.

Jeremy's palms were clammy. His throat was dry. Just a few more minutes alone together, that was all he needed. To talk to her. Find out if he was crazy for feeling like he did.

Jeremy reached out for Liv's arm. "Hey, Liv?"

But he was too late. She was already stepping out of the Celica.

And Patrick was already racing toward her.

"Liv!" Patrick's hair was even blonder from the summer sun, his skin smooth and tan. He let out a half scream, half whoop, and flung his arms around

Liv in the biggest bear hug Jeremy had ever seen.

Patrick pulled back then and stared searchingly into Liv's eyes. "Where were you guys?" he asked accusingly. "I've been going totally crazy here. We thought you must have been in some terrible car accident!" He touched Liv's cheeks and her arms, as if to prove to himself that she was indeed okay.

Liv shook her head and took his hand. "No, no, we're fine. We got lost on some no-man's road, and then we got a flat tire, and . . ." She trailed off. "Let's just say it was a long night," she finished. Her face glowed as she gave Patrick another hug.

By now Mr. and Mrs. Clark, Patrick's eleven-year-old sister, Shelby, and their golden retriever, Biscuit, had all run out of the house too. "Jeremy! Liv!" Mrs. Clark exclaimed, her hazel eyes filled with concern. She hugged them both tightly. "We were so worried about you two!"

"Sorry about that," Jeremy said, giving Mrs. Clark a quick kiss on the cheek. "Hey, Biscuit." He crouched down and gave the dog a brisk rub on the head. "Like Liv was just telling Patrick, we got a flat tire and we didn't have a spare, so we just had to wait for help to come."

"Which unfortunately didn't come until this morning," Liv added ruefully. "And I know Jeremy won't tell you this, but—"

Jeremy's heart skipped a beat.

"—it was kind of my fault that we didn't have a spare. Actually," she corrected herself, "it was completely my fault." She went on to tell them the story

65

of how she'd hidden the doughnut in the garage only to have her packing plan backfire on her.

Patrick squeezed Liv's hands. "Well, you had us majorly freaked out." He turned to Jeremy. "Thank God you were there, man." He clapped Jeremy on the back and then gave him a quick hug. "I wanted to come and look for you myself, but my parents wouldn't let me."

"Yeah," piped up Shelby. "Dad called the New Jersey state police, the Pennsylvania state police, and the New York state police!"

Jeremy laughed. "We weren't in New York, Shelby," he reminded her.

"See? That's how worried we all were," she answered, looking up at him adoringly. Jeremy gave her long blond ponytail a yank. Patrick's little sister was very cute, and she hung on every word Jeremy or Patrick said. She idolized her brother and his friends, especially Jeremy.

"Okay, everyone. Why don't we go in and have something to eat? Jeremy and Liv can call their families and let them know they're okay," Mrs. Clark said, motioning everyone to follow her up the walkway. Biscuit raced up to the staircase, barking excitedly.

"I second that," said Mr. Clark, grabbing Liv's suitcase, garment bag, and tote. "And you guys lucked out. It was overcast yesterday, but it looks as if today is going to be a prime beach day."

Shelby pulled Jeremy toward the house, talking a mile a minute. "You won't believe all the great stuff there is to do here," she told him excitedly.

"There's swimming and bicycling and beach volleyball and a sand castle contest, and . . ."

"Yeah?" Jeremy said, smiling down at her. She'd grown a little taller since he'd last seen her. He shuddered to think of what would happen in a few more years. She'd drive the boys crazy.

"Yep," Patrick contributed. He flung an arm around both Liv and Jeremy. "I've really missed you guys this summer. I've been counting the days down until you arrived." He turned to Jeremy. "So what's new? That grocery job sounded like the pits. Bagging groceries all day long would drive me insane."

Jeremy kicked a pile of gravel. "Well, not everyone has the luxury of lounging around the beach all day. Believe me, I'd much rather have spent my days surfing the waves instead of stocking the shelves," he joked.

Patrick frowned. "Hey, like I didn't do anything this summer? My mom has me running errands all day, and my dad's always drumming up some new project for me to work on. Check out those windows on the second floor," he said, pointing upward. "Installed by none other than Patrick the Great."

"More like Patrick the great beach bum," Liv teased, pinching his waist. "I can't believe how tan you've gotten. And your hair is even blonder than it was in June, which is hard to believe."

Patrick grinned down at her. "All natural, babe, all natural."

"There are so many cool people here this summer," Shelby burst out. Her eyes widened. "There are two boys my age, twins. And Lauren and Mallory—she's been in a ton of commercials—and there's a family from England too!"

"Is that so?" Jeremy remarked. But he was only half listening. Out of the corner of his eye he saw Patrick plant a soft kiss on Liv's cheek. She blushed. *She's so pretty,* Jeremy thought dejectedly.

"We've got some serious catching up to do," Patrick murmured, just loud enough for the words to reach Jeremy's ears.

Had Jeremy thought this girl could be someone special?

Well, sure she could.

Just not for him.

With a sigh Jeremy followed Shelby through the doorway into Pelican's Cove. Olivia Carlson was already taken. By his best friend. And the sooner he faced up to that miserable reality, the better.

Mrs. Clark put out a great spread on the large ceramic-tiled counter that overlooked the dining area: bagels with cream cheese; a bowl of nectarines, peaches, and grapes; homemade brownies; and an egg and ham strata. A plastic tumbler decorated with tropical fish was filled with pink lemonade, and a plain glass pitcher held ice water.

The conversation flowed easily, with the Clarks filling in Liv and Jeremy on everything that had gone on over the summer and eager for details of what had been happening back in Erie.

"How've your folks been?" Mrs. Clark asked,

helping herself to a bagel. "Did your mom's garden do well this summer?"

Jeremy nodded, wiping his mouth on a napkin. "We had more cucumbers and tomatoes than we knew what to do with. My dad was tempted to set up a vegetable stand right in front of our house."

He took a sip of lemonade. "And my mom wanted me to be sure and give you both their best." The Clarks and the Thomases, while not close friends, had developed a familiar bond. After years of shepherding each other's sons back and forth from Little League practice, Midget Football, junior-high-school dances, and now high school, their tie was inevitable—they'd watched their boys grow up together.

"That reminds me." Liv reached into her tote bag. "This is for you. Just a tiny thank-you for inviting me here."

"You didn't have to do that," Mrs. Clark said, accepting the package. "It's our pleasure."

"Well, it's not much," Liv said modestly.

The gift was a pair of wind chimes. "They're lovely!" Mrs. Clark said, giving them a little *plink* with her hands. They had a soft, musical peal. "Now, where to put them . . ." She motioned to Liv to follow her out on the deck, with Shelby right on their heels. "This might be a good place. . . ."

"It's good to see you, Jeremy," said Mr. Clark, getting up from the table. "Make yourself at home here."

"Thanks, Mr. Clark. I will."

Patrick leaned forward, his elbows on the table.

"Thanks for getting her here safely, Jere. I don't know what I would have done if she'd been hurt."

"It was no problem. I was glad to do it."

"Now there's something I've got to tell you. Something important." Patrick paused dramatically. "The bathroom is upstairs and to the right. Man, do you need a shower!"

Streaks of sunlight splashed across the moss-colored carpet as Patrick opened the door. He stood aside as Liv crossed the threshold.

"Oh, Patrick, it's lovely," Liv breathed. A large four-poster wrought-iron bed draped with swathes of gauzy white fabric lay covered with a white bedspread and piled with tiny pillows of different shapes and textures. A soft, lumpy green velvet chair sat opposite the bed, next to a small table graced with a crystal vase filled with white lilies and roses in full bloom. A heavy mahogany armoire was open, revealing twelve padded white satin hangers waiting for Liv's clothes to be hung on them. The room's large dormered window looked out onto the ocean, its curtains flapping gently in the breeze.

"I'm glad you like it," Patrick said, sounding pleased. He placed Liv's bags on the floor.

Above the bed hung a painting of a sand-dipped seashell, in pale peaches and soft lavenders. "That's so pretty," Liv commented, staring at it.

"My mom did it," Patrick told her. "She spends a lot of time in the summer painting. Cabinets, tables—old junk that other people throw away.

Every now and then she does a real canvas."

"She's really good."

"Yeah. I guess she is."

Liv moved over to the window and leaned out, her lips and tongue tasting the salty sea air. "I changed my mind. I don't like it here. I love it!" she exclaimed, turning from the window and smiling at Patrick. "You didn't tell me it would be like this," she said, gesturing at the bed, the painting, the window. It was so perfect.

Patrick's eyes lingered over Liv's body. "And you didn't tell me *you'd* look like this," he said, moving toward her. "I've missed you so much this summer, Livvie," he said, cupping her chin in his hand. "You don't know."

"Me too," said Liv, suddenly shy. She looked at Patrick, wanting to drink in every lean, tan feature she'd been missing all summer long. His tall, slim athletic body, tailor-made for rugby and lacrosse. His hair, always tousled, and his skin, soapy sweet.

Patrick's soft hazel eyes met her gaze with pleasure. *How could I ever have kissed Jeremy?* Liv thought, waves of guilt washing over her. She shook her head slightly, trying to block out the night before.

"This really is the best bedroom in the house," Patrick said slyly, flopping down onto the bed and dragging Liv along.

"Why's that?" she asked, sprawling beside him.

Patrick nibbled on Liv's ear. "Because it's right next to mine. So in case you get lonely at night, you won't have far to go," he whispered sexily. His hand moved down the curve of her waist.

"Patrick!" Liv swatted him. She could tell her cheeks were turning red, and she hated it. She and Patrick had done their fair share of fooling around, sure, but sex, well—she definitely wasn't ready for it, at least not yet.

Patrick brushed his fingers across her face. "Hey. I didn't mean to embarrass you or anything. No pressure, you know that. I'd never ask you to do anything you didn't want to do. When we're ready, we're ready. I—I just thought that maybe, well—" Patrick shrugged. "I'm just glad you're here," he finished. He leaned over and kissed Liv's lips.

"So am I," Liv whispered, burying her face in Patrick's tangled hair. Her mind speed-raced ahead to what the next few weeks together would bring. The last two weeks of the summer before senior year.

Crucial weeks. Weeks that would firmly cement them as a couple. Eating together. Talking together. Swimming together. Spending real time together. Growing closer. Bonding.

She closed her eyes and basked in the glow of being in Patrick's arms. Strong. Loving.

Secure.

EIGHT

Sunlight streamed through the bedroom window, hitting Jeremy squarely in the face. With a jolt he leaned over and attempted to turn off an imaginary alarm clock, his hand pawing the air. It was a routine he'd gotten to know well over the past few months.

Then it hit him. Today wasn't a sticky summer day in July. He wasn't in his non-air-conditioned room plastered with Pirates memorabilia and a poster of Teri Hatcher. There wasn't a spill in aisle 7. He was at Pelican's Cove. And he didn't have to worry about getting up. He grinned, savoring the thought. At last, after working like a dog all summer long, the last two weeks of summer would be pure nothingness. He didn't have to do anything if he didn't want to. He could just sit around and be a regular beach bum.

Jeremy pulled the sheet over his eyes to block

the sun. He was staying in Patrick's room, curled up under a mohair blanket in one of Patrick's twin beds. He wondered briefly if Patrick was awake, but he didn't have the energy to lift his head the two inches off the pillow to look. He rolled over and tried to fall back asleep.

But he couldn't. The events of the weekend came swirling back into his mind. For a brief moment Jeremy thought he had dreamed the whole thing. How could something like that have happened anyway?

Well, it did happen, Romeo. It was real. You kissed Patrick's girlfriend.

It wasn't even the act of kissing that was so bad. Not that it wasn't bad. It definitely was. What was so bad, really, were the feelings he'd been having before, during, and since it happened. It was like potato chips or something. He'd start off eating one. He knew they were bad for him, but he'd keep eating them. Pretty soon he'd have polished off the whole bag. But instead of saying, "Okay, now I'll eat something healthy, like celery or radishes or something," what did he do? He'd run out and buy another bag of potato chips.

That's kind of how it was with Liv. He knew she was bad for him. That he should run away and never look back.

Face it. The girl was toxic.

He should go find some nice, pretty, and most important, single, girl to like. But the problem was, Jeremy didn't want a celery stick.

74

He wanted a high-cholesterol salt-and-vinegar fat-filled potato chip.

Jeremy smushed his face down hard in the pillow, moving his body to a cooler spot on the tiny twin bed.

What a goof he was for kissing her. For even noticing her.

Jeremy tried to rationalize everything in his befuddled brain. His emotional mumbo-jumbo state of mind yesterday? That was just that—crazy hormonal thoughts that didn't mean a thing.

It was time to get his priorities straight. This was not Erie, Pennsylvania, home of the Seawolves baseball team and the U.S. *Brig Niagara*. No. *This* was the Jersey shore. The place to meet hot girls . . . girls he didn't have to commit to, girls who were single and free, girls who just wanted to have fun. *And that's all I want to do. Have fun. Relax. And sleep . . .*

Whump! A dull thud whipped Jeremy in the back. Slowly he lifted the covers. He'd been lobbed by the mother of all weapons. The Hacky Sack.

"Come on, already. Get up," Patrick said with mock annoyance, retrieving the Hacky Sack. He bounced it around on his knee. "It's going to be awesome out today. Some killer waves. Let's hit the beach!"

Jeremy squinted up at him. "Can't you hit it without me?" What time was it anyway?

Patrick gave the white miniblinds a sharp tug, filling the already sunny room with even more rays.

"Are you kidding me? I've waited for you to get here all summer, man. Now that you're here, do you really think I'm going to let you *sleep?*"

"Shhh." Patrick held a finger to his lips. "Liv's asleep. I didn't want to wake her."

Jeremy grimaced as he joined Patrick in the hallway after throwing a T-shirt on over his flannel boxers. "Thanks for showing me the same concern."

They ate breakfast out on the deck, a huge wooden structure that wrapped around the back of the house. Large wooden plant stands overflowing with impatiens and pansies sat on both sides of the glass doors that led inside to the kitchen and framed either side of the stairway that led down to the sandy beach below. Liv's chimes, hung beneath the bird feeder, tinkled merrily in the breeze.

Pelican's Cove was situated on a prime piece of oceanfront property, and the deck served as the perfect vantage point to see what was going on up and down the sandy stretch of beach. It was only nine-thirty in the morning, but the beach was beginning to fill up. Lifeguards were busy setting up their stations and putting up flags to indicate the swimming conditions. Families were arriving, plastic coolers and brightly colored beach towels in hand. It was a perfect August day.

"See the pier?" Patrick asked, waving a piece of bacon to the south.

Jeremy squinted. "Uh, barely." The only thing

he saw looked about the size of a Lego piece.

"It's a two-mile walk down there, two miles back. I've been jogging it at least three times a week." Patrick spread a huge glob of raspberry jam on his toast. "It's really good for the calves, jogging on the sand."

"Yeah, I guess it would be." Jeremy wasn't much of a jogger. He wasn't much of a morning person either. He needed a shower, breakfast, and last night's baseball scores, in that order. Only then was he ready to join the land of the living.

"I forgot, you're not worth much before ten," Patrick remembered aloud. "But I know what will wake you up." He tilted his head to the side. "There are some hot girls here this summer. Believe me, if I didn't already have such a terrific one, I'd have had a hard time choosing." He grinned slyly, wiggling his eyebrows up and down. "What kind of girl do you want to meet?"

Jeremy tilted back his chair. "I don't know. I guess someone fun. Pretty. The usual." He stared out at the ocean. "I guess I'll know when I see her."

Patrick frowned. "You're not still hooked on Krissy, are you?"

"Nah, she's history." That was over months ago. He hadn't bothered telling Patrick about the girl he'd seen a few times over the summer, Nicki Argent. Jeremy played on Millcreek's football team, and Nicki was in the pep squad. He'd run into one of her friends at the Dairy Queen this summer, and she'd told him that Nicki had a major crush on

77

him. Jeremy had always thought she seemed nice, so he asked her out.

That had been at the end of June. Nicki was nice, but after a while Jeremy began to feel trapped. When he had dated Krissy, the two of them gave each other plenty of space. But with Nicki it was different. She wanted to spend every moment of every day with Jeremy. After a month of feeling claustrophobic, Jeremy finally told her that he wasn't really into a commitment at the moment. That he needed to breathe.

She took it hard at first, calling him two or three times a day, riding her bike past his house, having her friends bug him during his shifts at the grocery store. But then Nicki's persistence paid off, sort of. Brock Kimmet, a guy who lived on the next block over, noticed Nicki riding her bike by one day and started talking with her, and pretty soon Jeremy was free.

It wasn't that Jeremy wasn't ready for a commitment. He could be. It just had to be the right girl.

The squall of seagulls jarred Jeremy from his thoughts, and he looked up, watching them swoop over the crests of sand that surrounded the house. He rubbed the sleep out of his eyes. "Hey, I think someone is trying to get your attention." Jeremy stood up.

Someone was standing on the deck of the house next door, next door being several hundred yards away. A girl with shoulder-length blond hair whipping in the wind waved.

Patrick looked over and waved back. "Oh, that's

Megan," he told Jeremy. "Her family has summered next to Pelican's Cove for years."

"Is she nice?" Jeremy asked. He wondered why Patrick had never mentioned her before.

"Yeah. Yeah, she is." Patrick leaned back in his deck chair. "It's funny, you know? I mean, I never really paid much attention to her. She's just a sophomore. But this year there's something different about her." He rubbed his chin. "And she really shaped up."

Jeremy looked back, but Megan had disappeared inside. "She didn't look young to me," he commented. "She looked kind of pretty."

Patrick sat up straight. "Aha! You've spotted the first girl you want to meet and it's not even lunchtime yet." Suddenly a grin spread across his face. "There she is."

Jeremy expected to see Megan bounding up the deck stairs. Instead it was Liv, carrying a carton of orange juice. She slid open the glass doors, joining them on the deck. "I can't believe I slept this late," she wailed, yawning as she poured herself a tall glass of juice. "So what's going on?"

"Jeremy's just been scoping out the action on the beach," Patrick informed her, his eyes twinkling.

"Is that so?" Liv said, glancing at Jeremy.

He shook his head. "Just because Patrick has always been a looker, he thinks that's all I'm interested in." He knew he sounded a little touchy, but he didn't want Liv to get the impression he was a flirt. That title had always belonged to Patrick.

Liv looked even more incredible than she had the day before. She was wearing an unbuttoned lavender shirt, revealing a lavender-flowered bikini top underneath. Cutoff jean shorts showed off her long, firm legs, and her feet were clad in brown leather thongs. Her toenails were painted a soft pale pink.

"You polished your toenails," Jeremy noticed. "They look nice."

Patrick glanced down at Liv's feet, then back at Jeremy. "'Her toenails look nice'?" He hooted. "When'd you become so foot observant?"

"I don't know," Jeremy said defensively, trying not to sound as dumb as he felt. "They just looked pretty, that's all."

"Enough about toenails," Liv interrupted, reaching for a piece of cold bacon. "I mean, we are eating here, right?"

"So what do you guys want to do today?" Patrick asked, polishing off his fifth piece of toast. "I could introduce you to some of the local surfers. They're really cool, especially the Boogie boarders. I've learned a lot." He grinned. "I'm not such a kelphead anymore."

"Kelp what?" Liv raised her eyebrows.

"A beginner. I can ride on my stomach and stand up now. We could go do some boarding, maybe head down the beach to Laguna Point. They've got killer waves there."

"Sounds cool," Jeremy said, nodding. Patrick definitely had the advantage when it came to water sports, but Jeremy could hold his own.

"Liv?" Patrick turned to her. "That sound okay with you?"

She shrugged. "Uh, sure. That sounds good."

There's no way she wants to spend the day as a threesome, Jeremy realized. *She wants to be alone with Patrick.* The idea of Patrick and Liv alone together made Jeremy feel slightly queasy. *But it shouldn't,* he thought, ashamed of himself. They were boyfriend and girlfriend, for Pete's sake. Jeremy had zero chance of ever hooking up with Liv again—and that's how it was supposed to be.

"Cool," Patrick said, oblivious to Liv's unenthusiastic tone. He looked pleased with himself. "Let me go get my trunks on and we're out of here."

Jeremy cleared his throat. "Hey, Patrick. Maybe this isn't such a good plan for today after all. I think Liv might want to do something else."

Patrick turned to Liv in surprise. "Yeah? Do you want to do something else? Just tell me, hon." He covered her hands with his. "I'll do whatever you want to do."

"This is what I want to do," Liv said, smiling up at him. "Why don't we head down to the beach— find a cool spot, and you two go boarding while I soak up as many rays as possible with my SPF 12."

"You're sure that's okay?" Patrick asked.

"Positive." Liv clapped. "You guys need to spend some time together without me hanging around all the time." She gave Jeremy a big smile. "And I think you got enough of me the other night to last a lifetime."

81

Jeremy's stomach did a little flip-flop. Who was she trying to kid? *I didn't get nearly enough of you the other night. Not for a thousand lifetimes.* That megawatt smile of hers was amazing. How could anyone have a smile like that . . . especially in the morning? Had she even brushed her teeth yet?

Jeremy glanced over at Patrick. He didn't seem to notice anything out of the ordinary in Liv's smile. But to Jeremy, it couldn't be more obvious. She was definitely flirting with him. A girl never smiled like that unless she was interested.

Jeremy turned to say something witty but was struck again by Liv's smile. She was doing it again.

The same gorgeous smile.

But this time the target of her affection wasn't him.

It was Patrick.

"We're going to have an awesome two weeks here, the three of us," Patrick said, grinning from ear to ear. "The two of you here makes my summer complete." He held up his half-full juice glass. "To us."

"To us," Liv said, clinking her glass against his.

"To us," Jeremy echoed. *To us.*

"Look at this one. It's so beautiful." Liv held up the fragile pale peach coral necklace. "I love it."

"It's nice," Jeremy said. The three of them were spending Tuesday afternoon at Canterbury Commons, an outdoor mall catering to the shore's tourist crowd. Little boutiques and craft shops lined the walkways, and vendors set up carts filled with various hair accessories, beachwear, and pottery.

"Yeah, it is," Patrick said, checking his watch. "I think you should buy it."

"Well . . ." Liv paused, fingering an amethyst-colored anklet. "I think maybe I'd rather look around for a while and make sure I don't see something else I like better."

Patrick sighed. "Look, Livvie, it's almost three o'clock. We've been here for almost two hours."

Liv placed the anklet carefully back on the counter. "Sorry. I guess I lost track of time." She curled her arm inside Patrick's. "What time is the art museum open until?"

"Don't tell me you're still planning on going to that old place?" Patrick exclaimed.

"Why not?"

"Yeah, why not?" Jeremy added. True, he was getting a little tired of the shopping scene, but he'd been kind of psyched to see the art museum. One of Mrs. Clark's paintings was on exhibit there this summer.

"Well, I told my friend Gavin we'd meet him down at the marina later today. I wanted to show you my dad's boat, and I promised Gav I'd help him clean up this old Sunfish he just got. It's getting kind of late to do everything."

Liv blinked. "Oh. Well, okay. The museum didn't matter that much to me anyway."

Jeremy tried to catch her glance, but she averted her eyes. *There's no way she means that.* He knew she'd spent an hour talking art with Mrs. Clark last night while he, Patrick, Shelby, and Mr. Clark had gone for a swim.

"Honey, if you want to go to the museum, we'll go," Patrick said softly, taking a strand of Liv's hair and letting it fall between his fingers. "It's not like I haven't been there at least twenty times with my mom already, but . . ." He touched her cheek. "I just want to make you happy. Gavin can wait."

"No. I'd like to see the marina and meet your friend," Liv told him. "Besides. It's not like the paintings are going anywhere, is it?" she said lightly.

"That's not likely." Patrick turned to Jeremy. "Is that cool, Jere? You didn't want to go to the museum or anything, did you?"

Jeremy shook his head. "I'm fine with going back to the beach, if that's what you guys want to do."

"It is," Liv said firmly, taking Patrick's hand.

"You really think you're going to go to Penn State?" Patrick asked Jeremy, wrapping his arms around Liv and pulling her into the easy chair near the fireplace. They had stayed in after dinner that night. Good thing too. It had rained like crazy for about ten minutes. A summer storm. Now it was just a slight trickle, pinging and panging in the tin gutters that surrounded the house.

Liv tried to turn her head to see Jeremy, but the angle made it impossible. She got up from Patrick's lap and sat on the footstool in front of the chair.

"Probably." Jeremy shrugged, stretching back on the couch. "I've liked what I've seen when we've been there with Mitchell. And the Nittany Lions are awesome." He looked extra-cute tonight, Liv thought guiltily, in his faded jeans and black T-shirt. Around his neck was a leather rope necklace he'd picked out at Canterbury Commons earlier in the day. It looked good.

"No doubt," Patrick said, reaching forward and massaging Liv's shoulder. She leaned away a little, discouraging him. She felt weird, having him touch her in front of his mom and Jeremy. It didn't feel right.

Ever since they'd gotten here, she'd felt a little guilty every time Patrick touched her. It wasn't that he didn't make her heart beat faster or anything like that, because he did. It was just that it felt different than it had back in May and June. Still good, but . . . she couldn't quite put her finger on it. Almost like something that had been there before was missing.

And in its place was her memory of Jeremy.

She shot Jeremy a dirty look. *It's all your fault, you adorable creep.* Why couldn't she stop thinking about him?

Mrs. Clark put down the book she was reading. "Penn State's a good school, especially if you don't know what you want to major in. There's such a big selection of classes there."

"Not everyone is as decisive as we are," Patrick said, giving Liv a squeeze. "My girlfriend the future drug dispenser."

"I think pharmacist is the more appropriate term, Patrick," Mrs. Clark said dryly.

Jeremy looked over at Liv. "Liv was telling me she'd had a change in plans. When we were in the car."

"Huh?" Patrick sat up. "Like what?"

"I don't know," Liv said shyly, frowning at Jeremy. He'd been superquiet all night long. Why did he suddenly have the urge to spill? "I've been kind of thinking that maybe I don't want to be a pharmacist."

"Are you kidding?" Patrick looked shocked. "You love science. It's the perfect job for you." He crossed his arms. "What do you want to do?"

Liv tucked in her knit top, which had popped out of her jeans. "Well, I've been thinking about going to veterinary school." She gave Biscuit a pat on the head.

Patrick snorted. "Veterinary school? Nice for you to tell me."

"I didn't realize I needed to run everything by you first," Liv said flatly, annoyed at his attitude. She couldn't believe how negative he was being. Jeremy had been totally supportive. *Like a* boyfriend *should be,* she thought angrily. "Anyhow, it was no big deal."

"Big enough for you to tell Jeremy, though."

"Vet, pharmacist, whatever." Mrs. Clark waved her hand in the air. "You all have plenty of time to decide what to do with your lives."

Patrick grabbed the remote and began flipping through the TV channels. "You're a whiz in chemistry, Liv. You shouldn't let that go to waste."

"You're right, Patrick. Chemistry is definitely

not to be ignored." Jeremy spoke up from the couch.

Liv glanced in Jeremy's direction and found his eyes fixed on her. She swallowed.

Chemistry.

NINE

LIV STUDIED HER reflection once more in the mirror. She was wearing her faded Calvin Klein overalls, with the new brown ribbed tank top she'd bought last week underneath. She piled her hair on top of her head. Should she put it up? No. Bad idea. The wind would just blow it down. She rummaged through her makeup bag and retrieved her brush, comb, and a brown velvet scrunchie. A French braid always looked neat.

"You look pretty."

Liv jumped. "You scared me!" she chided Shelby.

Shelby came into the room and stood behind Liv, staring at her reflection in the mirror. "Those are cool overalls," she said admiringly.

"Thanks." Liv wove the strands of hair in and out. People were usually surprised to hear that she could French-braid her own hair. It looked more complicated than it actually was.

"Mom and Dad never let me go to any of the beach parties," Shelby complained, busying herself with tying and retying the bow of a big stuffed teddy bear that sat on a little chair next to the bed. "They make such a big deal of everything."

"They just don't want you to get hurt," Liv told her, snapping the ponytail holder in place. She looked at the younger girl, who had now slumped forlornly on the bed.

"Hey. How about I give you a French braid too? Would you like that?"

Shelby's face lit up. "Sure! Then I'll look just like you. At least a little bit."

"We'll be twins," Liv promised. Shelby slid down onto the carpeted floor, and Liv began to brush.

"You know, Shelby," Liv mused, "you probably wouldn't like this kind of party anyway. It's just a bunch of teenagers acting goofy. I bet you'll have more fun staying inside and watching TV." Liv began to braid.

Shelby sighed. "Big whoop. You know what?"

"What?" Liv asked, continuing to fashion the braid.

"When I'm older, I'm going to have parties on the beach every night. And I'm going to stay up late, and I'm going to have my own telephone in my room so I can call all my boyfriends whenever I want."

"*All* your boyfriends?" Liv twisted her head around so her nose was almost touching Shelby's. "How many do you plan on having, Miss Clark?"

"Lots," Shelby answered airily. Then she frowned. "I'll never be able to decide on just one boyfriend. There are so many cute ones. How did you know that Patrick is the only boy you want to be with?"

Liv was silent for a few minutes. She finished the braid, snapped an elastic holder on, and tied a pale blue ribbon around the end.

"I'd never met anyone I liked any better than your brother," Liv answered truthfully.

Problem is, I hadn't met Jeremy yet.

"You look terrific," Patrick murmured, kissing Liv gently on the lips. They waved good-bye to Shelby, who stood pouting on the other side of the glass doors, and headed down the stairs to the beach. "I can't wait to introduce you to everyone," Patrick said. He pulled Liv by the arm. "C'mon."

Laughing, Liv allowed herself to be dragged through the sand, cool and damp beneath her toes. "You know I'm not going to remember anybody's name. I'm terrible with that sort of thing." She didn't like standing out in a crowd . . . she preferred to blend in, be one of the gang. But with Patrick that was impossible. Patrick was always where the action was.

"Remembering people's names doesn't matter. Just smile and act friendly. They'll love you." He stopped, wrapping his arms around Liv's waist. "Just like I do, Liv."

Liv felt her pulse race. Patrick had never said he loved her before.

Love. She'd fantasized having a guy say he loved

her, but actually hearing it was weird. *Love.* Just a word, but it made her feel pressure. Like she was expected to say something back. She gulped as Patrick's arms grew tighter around her waist.

"I love you," Patrick whispered, staring into her eyes.

"I—I—I heard you the first time," Liv stammered. Her face grew hot. She knew she was supposed to say, "I love you too," but somehow the words got stuck in her throat, and no matter how she tried, she couldn't get them out. Her palms were getting completely sweaty, and her mouth felt sandy. Not exactly how she'd pictured this scene in her head.

Patrick pulled back. "That's all you have to say?" he asked, surprised.

"A girl's got to keep some mystery involved," Liv answered lightly, breaking away toward the party scene ahead. "That's what keeps you guys coming back for more."

The party was about a quarter of a mile down the beach from Pelican's Cove. A huge pile of brush and sticks stood waiting to be lit, and a big stereo system was rigged atop a plywood board that sat squarely on an old tire. Loud rock music blared out over the beach. The oceanfront homeowners rarely complained. For one, lots of the kids out there were their own sons and daughters, and for two, the noise of the music tended to get drowned out by the crashing of the surf.

Liv was astonished to see how many people were already congregated there. "How many parties have you had here this summer?" she asked. Patrick's arm was slung casually over her shoulders.

"A lot. At least once a week. I kind of lost track. It just seems like we had one last night." The sound of R.E.M. came drifting toward them, the beat alternating with the endless crash of the surf.

The party definitely was much bigger than the ones Liv had been to in Erie. Had everyone under the age of twenty at Beach Haven shown up? Liv held on to Patrick's arm as they navigated through the crowd.

Then Patrick's eyes lit up in recognition. "Hey, there's my boarding buddies. Yo! Chris! Perry!" He waved to a couple of grungy-looking guys with Boogie boards standing down near the water. "You gotta meet these guys, Liv. They're really cool. Perry surfed the Banzai Pipeline in Hawaii last winter." He started toward them.

Liv hung back for a moment, her eyes scanning the crowd. "Wait a minute, Patrick. We told Jeremy we'd meet him down here. I don't think we should just leave him alone. That's not really very nice."

"Jeremy's a big boy, Liv. He can take care of himself." Patrick grinned. "And by the looks of things, he's doing a good job of it."

Liv followed Patrick's gaze. She recognized Jeremy's strong, muscular body, clad in a navy blue sweatshirt and jean shorts, immediately. His hair was wavier than usual, tumbling over his forehead in a mass of curls. To her surprise, Jeremy wasn't alone. He was standing with three girls, talking and laughing. One of them, a tall, leggy girl with cropped blond hair, leaned over and whispered in Jeremy's ear. Jeremy squeezed her shoulder and laughed. Liv frowned. He was laughing a little *too* hard. And who were those girls?

But why shouldn't he be laughing? she thought, fighting down the strange new possessive side of her that longed to run over and fling the girl's hand from his arm. *I told him I didn't want to be with him. That I was happy with Patrick.* She was happy with Patrick, she told herself sternly. So why did she feel as if her heart were twisting in two?

"Hi."

Jeremy turned. A girl with blond shoulder-length hair and gray eyes smiled back at him. She wore a pair of faded jeans and a cropped white T-shirt. He squinted. The girl looked vaguely familiar, but he couldn't quite place her. . . .

"My name's Megan. I live next door to the Clarks," she said, thumbing back toward Pelican's Cove. "I saw you out on the deck on Monday. That was you, wasn't it?"

"Yes. I knew I recognized you from some-where." Jeremy smiled. "We drove down on Saturday. Well, actually, it was Sunday." Jeremy shook his head. "Never mind. It's a long story. I'm Jeremy, by the way. Patrick's friend from back home."

"Hey, Jeremy, catch up with you later," April, the cropped blonde Jeremy had been talking to, called over her shoulder. She moseyed off, her two sidekicks right behind her.

Megan looked relieved to see them go. "Ugh! Those girls always latch on to whatever new guy is here. They're pathetic."

Jeremy laughed. "Now I really feel special."

"No, no! I didn't mean it like that." Megan giggled, blowing her bangs off her forehead. "They're just the local Beach Haven vultures, swooping down for a new victim." She grinned. "Patrick mentioned you were coming for a visit. You actually got here at a good time. A lot of the weekend summer crowds have thinned out. It can be a real pain sometimes. My dad had to kick people off our deck back in July. They got drunk and thought our house was a bar or something."

Jeremy laughed. "Sounds like they party hard here."

Megan nodded. "They definitely do. I never really used to hang out at night during the summer."

"Why?"

Megan's face flushed slightly. "I don't know. Just shy, I guess."

"Where are you from?"

"Philadelphia."

"That's pretty close, isn't it?" Jeremy asked.

"Yes. We're able to come here pretty much whenever we want during the rest of the year, unlike lots of the summer people," Megan explained.

"My parents like to come down on fall weekends when they have some free time. It's nice then."

"So where's your boyfriend? Back home in Philly?"

Megan kicked at a clump of seaweed. "I don't have one. Here or there."

"The guys here and there must be nuts," Jeremy told her sincerely. Megan was cute and seemed really sweet—Jeremy could think of a dozen guys back home who'd go for her.

"How about you? Do you have a girlfriend?"

Jeremy shrugged. "Nah. I'm just playing the field this summer."

"Oh." Megan cleared her throat. "Patrick and Liv are pretty serious, huh?"

Jeremy glanced over at the crowd, trying to locate Liv. "I guess you could say that. Patrick doesn't usually stay with one girl for very long."

"Really?"

Jeremy nodded. "He's kind of a Romeo. The partying type."

"Speaking of partying, do you want a drink or something? They've got beer and stuff, but I don't drink. Or sometimes I get myself a beer but end up holding it the whole night." She wrinkled her nose. "I still don't get why people like the taste of it so much."

"I'll get you something," Jeremy offered. "Maybe a Coke?"

Megan nodded, then changed her mind and shook her head. "Coke, yes. But I'll get it. Be right back!" She jogged off, her sneakers kicking up the sand as she ran.

95

Jeremy sat down, took off his sandals, and dug his feet into the cold, damp sand. The beach felt so different at night than it did during the day. It was hard to believe it was the same place. He felt something smooth underneath his toe. Reaching forward, he dug underneath the sand and pulled it out.

It was a piece of pale blue glass, worn smooth by years of exposure to the wind and sea. Someone had painted a tiny palm tree on it. He was about to stuff the glass in his pocket—Shelby would probably like it—when Megan came back, huffing and puffing. In her hands were two big plastic cups.

"Soda for me and punch for you."

"Punch?"

Megan nodded. "Some fruit punch somebody mixed up. They told me it's really good."

Jeremy sniffed the cup and took a tiny sip. "Is there alcohol in here? I don't smell any."

Megan shrugged. "I asked the guys mixing it up. They told me there wasn't really any in the punch, but that the fruit was soaked in it. If you want, I'll get you something else."

Jeremy looked in Liv's direction. He flinched as Patrick grabbed her from behind, tickling her. Liv was laughing, pushing Patrick away. They looked like they were having a hilarious time, tumbling back and forth across the sand. *Face it, Thomas. She's completely out of your grasp.*

"Punch sounds good right now." He took a big sip. "Just what the doctor ordered."

★　　★　　★

Jeremy shivered, pulling his sweatshirt close to his body. He was alone now . . . Megan had drifted away to talk to a group of people. He didn't feel very good. His stomach felt queasy, as if it were tied up in a hundred knots. And his head was beginning to ache terribly. *Is that the surf pounding or my head?* he wondered wearily. He lay back, the damp sand tickling his bare neck and legs. The world was spinning, faster and faster. He tried to sit up, but a wave of nausea spilled over him.

Jeremy turned his head and threw up. *Must have been the punch,* he thought, dazed. He managed to sit himself up and, after a few seconds, stood up. *Just get back to the beach house. Lie down.*

He stumbled forward, hoping that no one saw him but not really caring if they did.

But he'd stood up too fast. As another wave of nausea hit him Jeremy gasped, holding his stomach. He doubled over and vomited.

Sick. Got to get back to the house.

He threw up again.

"Jeremy!"

Suddenly Liv was there, holding him.

"Ooh, a little too much punch, I think," she said softly.

"That shrimp and scallop paella we had for dinner didn't help me any," he croaked, groaning at the thought of it.

"Can you make it back to Pelican's Cove?" she asked.

Jeremy managed to nod. "I think so."

"Okay, then." Liv held up her hands. "I'm going to go tell Patrick we're leaving. I'll be right back. You sit right here." She eased him down. "Don't move."

"Don't worry." He knew he looked pretty bad, but he was too sick to care.

Liv raced back to the bonfire. The blaze was huge, throwing a tremendous wave of heat on the onlookers.

"Have you seen Patrick Clark?" she asked a couple of guys wearing Temple University sweatshirts.

"No, but you can stay and talk to us."

Liv gave them a clipped smile. "Thanks anyway, guys." She made her way through the crowd. There were so many people there. *It doesn't make any sense. We've got the whole beach, and everyone is clumped into one giant mass.* It was really hard to distinguish faces in the velvety black air.

A short, muscular guy wearing khaki-colored shorts and a white T-shirt bumped her arm, spilling his too-full beer glass down her leg.

"Sorry, babe," he said, his words slurred. His eyes looked glassy and round. "You wanna party with me?" Liv recoiled from the guy's hot, beer breath smell. She felt warm and sticky. Panicky. She pushed past the guy without speaking. Big crowds of people intimidated her. *Where's Patrick? He'll know what to do.*

Then she spotted him, standing in a group of guys and girls, talking and laughing. Liv felt her temper flare. *How can he stand over there having a good time? Doesn't he even wonder where I am? He wasn't concerned at all.* She began to move through the crowd toward him.

But then she hung back. *She* was the one who had encouraged him to enjoy himself while she stayed back on the fringes and talked to some people she'd met Monday on the beach. *It's not Patrick's fault,* she thought guiltily. She watched him. He looked like he was having a really good time. People always gravitated toward Patrick. It was a given that he was the life of any party.

"So then the guy says, 'And thank *you* for the blue Popsicle!'" Patrick's voice came in loud and clear—and so did the laughter that followed his punch line.

Patrick's just being . . . Patrick. I don't need to interrupt his good time just to walk us back to the house. Besides. She patted her pocket. Mrs. Clark had insisted she have her own set of keys to Pelican's Cove while she was there. She wanted Liv to come and go as she pleased.

Patrick wouldn't miss her. She'd be back before he'd even noticed she was gone. *He'll still think I'm over there roasting marshmallows.*

Liv turned on her heel and ran back to where she'd left Jeremy. Seeing Jeremy's big green eyes so weak and helpless had made her feel protective.

She couldn't just leave him alone like this. The thought occurred to her that she could ask someone else to take him back. But she pushed it out of her head.

Right now, Jeremy was her responsibility.

And for some reason, she was glad he was.

They began to walk slowly up the beach, Jeremy leaning on her right shoulder. "Easy now. One step at a time," Liv coached gently.

Jeremy grimaced, his hand on his stomach.

"Are you going to get sick again?" Liv stepped back.

"No. I'm fine," he muttered.

Then he threw up all over his sandals.

Thankfully, Mrs. Clark had left the back deck lights on. They made a tremendous noise climbing up the stairs—Jeremy's feet slamming on board after board, Liv trying to shush him—but finally Liv figured out how to get the door unlocked and they were safely inside. Liv eased Jeremy down on the couch.

"I'll be right back," she whispered, hurrying into the kitchen. She returned with a huge wad of wet paper towels and began dabbing at Jeremy's face. His eyes were closed.

"You have the longest eyelashes I've ever seen on a guy," she murmured, wiping his forehead. "It's not fair."

A little moan escaped his lips. "Thanks, Liv. For helping me." He struggled to get the words out.

"Shhh," she whispered, touching his cheek. "You sleep now. You'll feel much better in a few hours. I promise." She stared down at him. Even when he was sick, he looked cute. Sweet and defenseless. He'd started to sweat, and his hair was stuck to his forehead in tiny sweaty clumps. Little beads of sweat had broken out above his lip. She wiped them with a paper towel.

Liv realized that this was the first time they'd been alone together since the car trip. The memory of what had happened that night came flooding back to her . . . the soft touch of Jeremy's lips on hers. Then she shivered. Liv could never, ever let a moment like that happen again. And the fact that she'd even thought about it at all made her feel small and mean. No matter how she felt, she couldn't betray Patrick's trust.

She wouldn't.

Jeremy opened his eyes. *Where am I?* The TV was playing softly, throwing a cast of light over the room. A light wool throw covered his legs, and his sandals were placed neatly under the coffee table.

"How are you feeling?" The soft female voice from behind his head startled him.

Liv. "What time is it?" Jeremy mumbled.

"Oh, about 1 A.M.," Liv answered.

"Have you been in here the whole time?"

She nodded, getting up from her spot on the rocking chair. "You were in no condition to be moved, and I was afraid if I left you, you'd fall off the couch or go crashing through the glass doors and really hurt yourself." She peered worriedly into Jeremy's pale face. "Can I get you something?

Pepto-Bismol? Some Tums? How about some ginger ale?" She smiled encouragingly. "That always makes me feel better when I'm sick."

"Okay," Jeremy said weakly. He felt a bit better now than he had before. The dizziness had stopped, and his stomach had given up its endless round of gymnastic flip-flops.

Liv walked over to the kitchen, which overlooked the family room.

"Hey, aren't you missing the party?" Jeremy croaked, massaging his throbbing temple. "You should be out there with Patrick and everybody."

Liv shrugged, cracking open a can of soda. "Patrick's okay without me," she said, walking back in. She handed Jeremy a glass and sat down at the end of the couch. "Besides, I was getting kind of cold out there. And I don't really like being at parties where I don't know anyone."

"Yeah. I know how you feel." Jeremy moved his legs and sat up. It was a bit scrunched with him lying there all sprawled out. "Thanks for helping me before. I—I really appreciate it."

Liv was silent. "You should be more careful," she said finally. "Seafood, the sun, and alcohol punch don't mix."

Jeremy winced. "Don't remind me." On the television an image of a guy and girl, laughing, walking down a beautiful European-looking street, flicked on the screen. They looked like they were really into each other. "What are you watching?"

"*Before Sunrise.* With Ethan Hawke and Julia

Delpy?" She sighed. "It's so romantic. Ethan plays this guy named Jesse. He meets Celine, played by Julia, on this train that's going through Austria, and the two of them fall in love after spending the day together in Vienna."

"Just one day, huh?"

"Mm-hmm. They decide that they're not going to keep in touch afterward, but their passion is so strong that they can't keep apart, and they agree to meet in Vienna next year."

"Well, I guess it's almost over, then," Jeremy said, taking a sip of ginger ale.

"No! I've just seen this about four times. That's how I know what happens." She grabbed a few M&M's from the glass candy dish that sat atop the coffee table and popped them in her mouth. "I'm more of a movie and museum person than a party person."

"Good thing. Thanks again for coming to my rescue."

Liv tickled his foot, sending a small zap of unexpected pleasure through Jeremy's body. "Will you stop thanking me already? It was my civic duty to make sure you were okay." She curled back. "Besides. Who needs a party when you've got such stimulating entertainment right here in the Clark family room?"

Jeremy smiled weakly. "I must look totally disgusting."

Liv patted his calf. "No. You just look exhausted. What were you drinking that stuff for anyhow? That alcohol punch is lethal."

Jeremy covered his ears. "Don't say that word. Ouch." He smiled. "I know what you mean about parties. Patrick always drags me to them—he loves a good time. But I guess I don't need to tell you that about Patrick. You know him pretty well already," Jeremy finished.

"You'd think so, right?" She twirled a loose strand of hair around her finger. "I thought I did, but . . ."

"But what?"

Liv took a deep breath and then let it out slowly. "I don't know. I mean, don't get me wrong. I really, really, *really* like Patrick. He's a terrific boyfriend. But sometimes I think that maybe I don't know him very well at all."

Jeremy wondered if this was a good idea. Talking about Patrick behind his back made him uneasy. He'd already betrayed him once. He didn't want to do it again.

"We have a good time together, but I catch myself wondering if we're having just a good time or a boyfriend-girlfriend kind of good time." Liv lined up a row of M&M's on the table. "If we're meant to be with each other. It's like—" She broke off. "We get along great in so many ways, but sometimes I feel like we're on different planets or something."

Liv shook her head ruefully. "Like right now, Patrick is out there surrounded by a million people, telling some funny story. But I'd rather be inside, curled up in here. Patrick always wants to be where the action is. But I don't." She fingered the metal loop that held up her overalls. "That's not really me."

"That's not what I heard. Aren't you Miss Popularity at Lincoln High?" Jeremy teased.

Liv's face flushed a deep crimson. "See, that's exactly how Patrick thinks. I've got friends. So? Is that a crime?"

Jeremy held up his hands. "Whoa. Easy, easy."

"No. You don't get it. Just because I've got a lot of friends doesn't mean that I *want* to be the center of attention." Liv chewed the inside of her lip. "I don't want attention, but it finds me. Patrick wants it. That's the difference."

"That doesn't mean you guys aren't right for each other, though. Just because you date someone doesn't mean you have to be just like them," Jeremy said, in a voice that he hoped sounded reassuring. He'd made a vow to himself that he would not sabotage Liv and Patrick's relationship—if anything, he'd try to make it stronger. His friendship with Patrick meant too much. Jeremy couldn't risk it for an unsure thing like love.

Liv nodded. "I know. But it's not just that. Like, hanging out and stuff. When we were back in Erie, before summer, I'd see Patrick usually one night during the week, and on the weekend we'd do something, like get a pizza or go to a movie. But here, seeing him every day . . ." She trailed off. "It's different," she said finally. "A little scary."

"Just think how it is when you're married."

Liv shuddered. "I don't know if I'll ever get

married. I'd rather stay single forever than end up with some loser I don't love. Not that Patrick's a loser," she added hastily. "You know what I mean." She threw her hands over her mouth. "I'm sorry. I shouldn't be telling you all this."

"Hey, I'm glad you did," Jeremy told her. And he meant it. He reached over and gave her a hug. She smelled faintly of coconut suntan lotion and salt water, and her cheek was warm and soft against his own slightly stubbled cool one.

If I could just touch her once more. He fought the urge to move his hands up her spine, her back, to her slender exposed neck. A neck that was just waiting to be kissed. . . .

He didn't need to fantasize about how it would feel to kiss Liv's soft, strawberry-colored lips. He'd already kissed them. He knew.

And despite everything, he had to admit he wanted to know again. Jeremy felt lower than scum. He'd never been like this before. If someone had told him he'd fall for Patrick's girlfriend, he'd have laughed long and hard in their face.

"Thanks for listening, Jeremy," Liv said gratefully. She pulled away. "You're really sweet."

Sweet. Just what he wanted to hear.

Liv moved her hand over and put it on top of Jeremy's. Her violet eyes clouded. "About before? I wasn't trying to hint or anything about, um, you and me." She looked embarrassed. "This is something between me and Patrick."

"Yeah. I know." Jeremy leaned back, trying to

look casual. He'd meant what he said . . . he wanted to be there for Liv. Listen to her. Help her out if he could. But he couldn't deny the fact that part of him (the disloyal, friend-betraying part) hoped that things didn't work out between Liv and Patrick.

Because then maybe I could have a chance with her. We wouldn't be hurting anyone. It would be okay.

He'd been wrestling with his feelings for the past few days. Back and forth, back and forth. Part of him said to forget the whole thing. How could he stab his best friend in the back by going after Liv? But feeling the way he felt, it would be a lie to go out with anyone else.

On the TV screen Jesse and Celine began to kiss madly.

It was just a movie. Real life didn't happen that way.

But Jeremy knew that it was possible to fall in love in just one day. He was absolutely, totally convinced.

Because it had happened to him.

TEN

"I LOVE IT out here."

Patrick ran his hand through the water, surprisingly clear after a choppy morning. "It's pretty awesome, isn't it? Beats being in some cruddy old study hall at Millcreek, that's for sure."

The guys had spent an intense morning Boogie boarding. The waves had been just right, steady, giving them enough speed to make about fifteen successful runs. Now, as the sun slipped its way across the sky, they were floating on the Clarks' bright canvas-covered rafts. The water was much calmer now, and they were out past where the waves did any real damage.

"You're not really supposed to come out this far," Patrick said. "But the lifeguard knows me. He's cool."

Jeremy wrapped his arms around the raft and closed his eyes. It was so peaceful out here. He felt like he could float forever.

"Hey." Patrick nudged Jeremy's raft with his toe. "You're so quiet. You're not feeling sick again, are you?"

Jeremy shook his head. He'd fallen asleep last night on the couch. When he woke up, it had been close to noon. Patrick and Liv had gone for an early morning bike ride along the parkway. When they'd returned, Patrick had dragged Jeremy out to the beach, Liv insisting she'd find something to do on her own.

"If I had known how sick you were, I definitely would have left the bonfire, man. I felt terrible this morning when Liv told me what a wreck you were last night."

Guilt jabbed him in the gut, a feeling that was becoming disconcertingly familiar. "I'm glad you didn't leave. You couldn't have helped anyway. I just needed to lie down."

Patrick paddled, propelling himself farther out into the ocean. "So what do you really think of her?" he asked, resting his chin on the raft.

"Who? Liv?"

"No, my mom. Yeah, Liv, dufus. Who else?"

Yeah. Who else. "She's really nice." *And she's a great kisser too.* Jeremy cringed. *Yes. I am a slime.*

"She's more than nice. She's awesome. She's got a body that won't quit, a beautiful face, and to top it off, she's sweet. What's not to love?"

"Love?"

"Well, not *love*." Patrick looked embarrassed. "You know, though. I mean, she's hot. You can't tell me you haven't noticed."

109

"I've noticed." Jeremy slid off the raft, cooling himself in the water. It felt incredibly refreshing and quiet. He wished he had worn his goggles. He loved looking at the ocean life that teemed under the surface. It was a different world down there. He lingered under the surface for as long as he could hold his breath, then burst to the top.

He swam over and retrieved his raft, which had floated to the south. "But there's more to life than just being hot," Jeremy muttered, climbing back on.

Patrick gave him a quizzical look. "Since when?"

"You know what I mean. When you first like a girl, sure, her body is what attracts you. But then when you get to know her as a person, it changes."

"Like how?"

"I don't know. Like you get to know personal stuff. Stuff that brings you closer together."

Patrick grinned. "Well, Liv wears a 34B. That brings me closer."

"I'm serious, Patrick. There's more to Liv than just her looks. She's an interesting person."

A look of annoyance flashed across Patrick's tanned face. "Ever since the road trip you act like you're an expert on my girlfriend."

"I'm not saying I'm an expert," Jeremy said evenly. "I'm just saying she's not just some . . . girl. She's, uh, special." Jeremy halted as he spoke the words. *Patrick is going to think that I've completely lost it.*

"You don't need to tell me that. I know she's special. *That's* why she's my girlfriend," Patrick said

110

defensively. "We tell each other everything. There's nothing about her I don't know."

"So then I guess you know all about Joe and her mom and stuff," Jeremy said. He couldn't resist. He knew it was kind of jerky, but Patrick's attitude was annoying him. Patrick had an awesome girlfriend, yet he barely seemed to know her.

"What? What's there to know? Liv's dad split when she was ten, and now her mom is seeing this guy."

Eleven. "Yeah, a guy she can't stand."

"Joe?" Patrick looked confused for a moment. He splashed some water on his arms and back. "She's never said anything bad about him to me."

Maybe you never asked, thought Jeremy. It wasn't like Patrick was a noncaring guy or anything. He was one of the most concerned, ready-to-help people Jeremy had ever met. He just tended to focus on what he wanted to focus on. Being with Liv was one thing. Dealing with her whole family life—well, that was something else.

"You know. Just that Liv doesn't like him hanging around all the time, that's all." Jeremy started to think that maybe he should keep his mouth shut. He didn't have any business discussing Liv's personal life out here in the middle of the Atlantic.

"I guess she might have said something about it, now that you mention it," Patrick mused.

"Or maybe she didn't," Jeremy said under his breath as he drifted away. "Maybe she only shared that with me."

★   ★   ★

111

"Hey, Liv!"

Liv shaded her sleep-deprived eyes and looked in the direction of the voices. She'd stayed inside and read for a while—one of the books on her summer reading list that she hadn't gotten around to reading yet—but the lure of the warm summer sun was too much to resist. A group of three girls were sprawled out on their stomachs on an old faded bedsheet, which was covered with beach towels and tote bags.

"Come on, join us!" they called.

Liv took off her thongs and maneuvered her way across the beach blankets that dotted the sand. It was Laura and Joyce—she'd met them at the party. And she recognized the shoulder-length blond-haired girl in the black suit too. She was the one who had been talking with Jeremy.

They scooted over to make room for her.

"Beautiful day, huh?" Laura said. She gestured to the blond girl. "Did you guys meet last night? This is Liv, Patrick Clark's girlfriend. Liv, this is Megan Pirelli. Her house is right next door to Patrick's."

Liv smiled. "Hi."

"Hi." Megan smiled back. "I've heard a lot about you."

Liv made a face. "Only good stuff, I hope."

"Only good stuff," Megan replied, her cool gray eyes checking Liv out. Was it Liv's imagination, or did she sense a certain distrust in Megan's tone? Oh, well. She shook it off. She'd just met the girl. There wouldn't be a reason for her to dislike her.

"So where are the guys today?" Joyce asked, adjusting the strap on her green tie-dyed bikini top.

"They're out boarding. Patrick and I went for a bike ride this morning, so I thought I'd let them be alone for a while, do some guy stuff."

"Wow. I don't know if I'd let two gorgeous guys like that slip out of my sight for one minute." Laura sighed. "I would kill to be in your sandals. You get to stay in the same house as those two."

Liv laughed. "It's a tough job, but someone has to do it."

Just then two women in their twenties wearing neon-colored thong bikinis pranced by them.

"That is what gives Jersey girls a bad name," griped Laura, making a face as the guys around them ogled the pair. "Butt cleavage is something I don't need to see before lunchtime."

"Tacky city," Megan added.

"Those boobs were definitely pumped up with silicone," muttered Joyce. "And please. If I hear one more person say a thong is comfortable, I'll strangle them with one."

Megan, Laura, and Liv laughed. It felt good to be with girls again, Liv realized. She hadn't phoned any of her friends at home since she'd left. And her closest friends, Rebecca and Hayley, were both away on vacation with their own families. These new girls couldn't take their place, of course, but it was a refreshing break from the guyspeak she'd been surrounded with.

They filled Liv in on all the beach gossip. Just as

it was getting juicy, two dark shadows fell across their backs.

"May I take your order, ma'am?" Patrick and Jeremy stood there, grinning. Patrick took out an imaginary check pad and waited. The guys had come straight from the ocean to drip over them—and see if they wanted anything from the Burger Shack.

"Is there anything healthy on the menu?" Liv asked, going along with the game.

Patrick looked up at the sky, pretending to be deep in thought. "Well, let's see. We've got greasy ribs; fat, juicy burgers; deep-fried chicken fingers; and, let's not forget, chicken wings with extra-spicy hot sauce. All with fries or onion rings, of course. And don't forget our fat-free condiments."

"Well . . . does anyone want to split anything?" Liv asked.

Joyce and Laura shook their heads. "We're going to the mall later with Laura's mom," Joyce said. "I think we're going to eat at the Chili's that's over there."

Megan shrugged. "If you want to share the honey-dipped chicken fingers, they're good. . . ."

"And an order of onion rings?" Liv finished. Megan nodded.

"That's it, then," Liv said. "And a diet Coke."

"Make that two," Megan added.

The Burger Shack, Beach Haven's best source of decent and cheap burgers, was about a mile south of Pelican's Cove. You could get there on the street, or you could walk along the shore and access it directly from the beach.

"Did you hear that?" Jeremy asked, clapping a hand to his growling stomach as they headed down the beach. "I had no idea I was so hungry."

"Being on the water always does that to you. It's the ocean air or something," Patrick said.

The beach was filled to capacity today, due both to the excellent weather and to the fact that there were only a few days left in August before the official end of the season on Labor Day weekend. It was a real scorcher too, despite the breeze that slid easily off the ocean. Jeremy was glad his mom had insisted he bring waterproof sunblock.

They walked by a group of well-built girls clad in skimpy bikinis sitting on beach towels. "Hi, Patrick," four female voices called out in unison. Patrick stopped.

"Hi. How's it going?" he said. The girls beamed back at him. "This is Claire, Kelly, Lisa, and Didi," he said, pointing to each girl from left to right. Then Patrick slung his arm around Jeremy. "This is my buddy Jeremy from Erie. He's down here for two weeks."

Jeremy smiled politely. Patrick knew more girls down here than Jeremy knew back home. "Nice to meet you."

"We saw your girlfriend last night, Patrick," Kelly said casually. She poured some lotion on her legs and began to rub it in. "She didn't stay for long, though, did she?"

"No. She, uh—"

"It was my fault," Jeremy cut in. "I wasn't feeling well, and she made sure I got back to the house okay."

"How sweet." Kelly turned to Patrick and pouted. "So I guess we're not going to be going to the movies anymore this summer." She toyed with her wavy brown hair. "The good ones are always taken," she whispered to Lisa, loud enough for them all to hear.

Patrick gave Kelly a small smile. "Summer's almost over anyway. Back to the real world."

The girls grimaced and nodded.

"Well, it's been nice seeing you guys. Be cool."

The sand was burning hot under their toes, and they walked back down toward the water to cool them off. "What was she talking about, going to the movies?" Jeremy asked, picking up a tiny horn-shaped shell. He flung it out into the ocean.

Patrick shrugged. "We went to the movies a couple times this summer together. It was no big deal."

Jeremy glanced at Patrick. "You guys dated?"

Patrick snorted. "Please. I've got the most awesome girlfriend in the world. I'm not about to cheat on her. Kelly and I just ended up hanging out together a couple of times, and we saw a few movies. So what?"

Jeremy shrugged. "Does Liv know?"

"No, she doesn't. Why would I tell her? She'd just get mad, and there's nothing to get mad about." Patrick reached down to wet his hands in the water and ran them through his hair. "You can't tell girls everything. They go ballistic for no reason at all."

They reached the takeout window of the Burger Shack and got in line behind a sand-covered group of kids and a harried-looking mom.

"You know a lot of girls here," Jeremy commented.

Patrick tapped his chest. "It's hard to be modest when you're a stud like myself. So many girls, so little time."

"But it's not like you've done anything with any of them, right?" Jeremy asked in a low voice.

Patrick gave Jeremy a playful shove. "Are you kidding? I told you. Of course not. I—"

"Hi, Patrick!" Two girls on in-line skates waved from across the street. "Who's your friend?" one of them, a tall, thin girl, called out teasingly. She had long black hair and wore black spandex shorts and a blue bikini top.

Patrick grinned. "Why don't you stop by my house later on, Taylor, and find out?"

The girls slowed down, as if they were toying with the idea of coming over. "Maybe we will," the girl named Taylor said provocatively. Laughing, they skated away.

Patrick looked at Jeremy, his eyes twinkling. "See? It just happens. I'm a girl magnet."

Jeremy had to laugh. Flirting came as naturally to Patrick as waking up in the morning and stretching. It wasn't his intent; it was his nature.

★　　★　　★

"You were so lucky to have been trapped in the car with him for twenty-four hours," Laura said enviously. "He was telling us about it last night."

Liv wondered exactly how much Jeremy had told. *That's silly, though. He didn't tell them anything. Like we agreed, it didn't happen.*

Joyce nudged Laura. "Liv already has a boyfriend, dodo."

Laura laughed, dabbing some lip balm on her lips. "I know, I know. But still. Jeremy is so cute. He's got the prettiest eyes. They remind me of Brad Pitt's."

"Brad Pitt has blue eyes," Megan reminded her.

"I know. I just mean his eyes are so beautiful, they're on Brad Pitt's level. That's all. And did you see how his butt looked in those swim trunks?" She closed her eyes. "I'll be dreaming about it the rest of the week."

"You're so bad," Joyce reprimanded. "But I have to agree!" Everyone giggled. "And he's so sweet," Joyce added. "When I had to go to the bathroom last night during the party, he walked me up to the public rest rooms to make sure I was safe and okay."

"That is *so* sweet," Laura marveled.

"I know," Joyce said emphatically. "Do you think any of the duds *I* date would ever think to walk me to the bathroom? They'd tell me just to use the ocean or something."

The other girls made faces of disgusted agreement.

"He was really nice to me last night too," Megan said. "I could actually sit and have a conversation with him and feel like he was interested in what I was saying."

A little pang of jealousy fluttered in Liv's stomach. She felt protective of Jeremy. He wasn't hers, but then again, he was. Wasn't he? She didn't like hearing other girls dissect him like he was some movie star open to public scrutiny. He was Jeremy. Her Jeremy. They only thought they knew how sweet he was. *I really know. The way he kissed me on Saturday night, all doe-eyed, soft and sweet. . . .*

"Okay, girls, time to flip," announced Joyce, looking at her Swatch. "We've been lying on our stomachs for exactly thirty minutes."

They flipped.

"So does he have a girlfriend at home?" Laura asked Liv.

"Yes, he does. So stay as far away from him as possible." That was what Liv wanted to tell her. But she didn't. Instead she found herself saying, "Well, uh, I don't really know for sure. I don't think he does. It's, um, hard to say. He's kind of quiet about things."

"He doesn't," Megan informed them. "I asked him."

Liv turned her head in surprise. Was Megan interested in Jeremy?

"I noticed you went off with Jeremy last night, Liv," Megan said, her voice calm. "Was everything okay?"

"Not at first. He got really sick from some punch he drank. That, combined with the seafood we had for dinner, made for a bad scene." Liv slipped on her new pair of silver Oakley sunglasses to block out the sun glare. "I couldn't find Patrick and I couldn't leave Jeremy throwing up on the beach, so I took him back to the house."

A look of blame appeared on Megan's face. "Punch? I—I brought him that punch. I didn't know that's why you guys left. I thought that—" She stopped, her cheeks pink.

"Thought what?" Liv prompted.

Megan shook her head. "I—um, nothing, I guess. I think I'm going to go cool off before the food comes." She stood up, made sure her suit covered her crucial areas, and ran down to the water.

"What was that all about?" Liv asked the others. "Am I the only one who's a little confused here?"

Laura sighed. "Megan has had a major crush on, uh, this guy for years. She lost a lot of weight this past year, and I think she was planning on coming to Beach Haven this summer and really knocking his socks off."

"But then when she got here, she found out that he had, um, a girlfriend now, and it kind of put a monkey wrench into everything," Joyce added, glancing at Laura.

"So what does this have to do with Jeremy?" Liv asked.

Laura picked up a fistful of sand and let it seep through her fingers. She sighed. "Well, we might as well tell you. The guy Megan likes is Patrick."

A surge of relief ran through Liv. *She's not after Jeremy.*

"Don't get mad, Liv," Joyce urged, biting her lip. "Megan is really nice. She'd never do anything behind your back. I just think that when you left with Jeremy last night, she was kind of hoping that you were doing something with him you shouldn't be, and that maybe you and Patrick were having problems or something."

Liv sat up and leaned back on the palms of her hands. "Oh." For some reason, knowing this didn't make her angry or anything. If anything, she felt indifferent. *This is a bad sign,* she told herself. *Indifference is bad.*

"And now when she sees how incredibly beautiful and nice and sweet you are, it makes her feel even worse," Laura told her. "But don't worry. Nothing's gone on with them at all. Trust me. Patrick's been completely faithful. He's talked about you all summer. And Megan's not the type to start anything with someone else's boyfriend."

All summer. All summer long, Liv had talked about Patrick to anyone who would listen: her friends, her mother, even her dog.

It was funny.

Because now that she was here, she didn't want to talk about him at all.

"Number 67, your order is ready. Sixty-seven, your order."

The guy behind the counter handed them two flimsy cardboard boxes filled with the food and drinks.

"All I'm trying to say is that you've got a great girlfriend and you shouldn't go around doing things that might screw it up," Jeremy finished uncomfortably. He didn't know what to say or what to do. He felt like an imposter of his normal self. Things were all wrong. This pleasure trip to the shore was turning into a big fat guilt trip. No way did he want to come between Patrick and Liv. But he couldn't stop thinking about her. It was driving him crazy.

"I appreciate your advice, but I don't need you to tell me how to handle being in a relationship," Patrick said, a tinge of annoyance coloring his words. He grabbed the ketchup bottle and squeezed a big blob onto his cheeseburger. "Do I have to remind you that I'm the one who's *in* a relationship? It's like, I'm Paul Reiser. I've got my Jamie. You're still Johnny, the single guy, last time I checked."

Jeremy opened his mouth to answer but checked himself instead. Patrick was right. It wasn't his place to tell Patrick how to deal with Liv.

With a sigh he took a bunch of napkins, some straws, and a couple of the relish packets in the bin on the counter and followed Patrick back down to the beach. He and Patrick had always talked about everything. If he liked a girl, Patrick was the first to know. They didn't share every intimate little detail of a crush or a date—after all, they weren't girls or anything—but Jeremy was used to confiding in

122

Patrick. He'd been doing it for eight years.

Now his life was speeding down a different road. And Jeremy felt powerless to put on the brakes.

"I need something nice for a girl. A friend of mine," Jeremy awkwardly informed the saleswoman after looking around the shop for fifteen minutes. He wanted to get a thank-you gift for Liv. A token of appreciation for helping him out last night. He'd spotted the tiny jewelry shop earlier and had slipped out of the house while everyone was showering for dinner. But nothing he saw was right.

The woman thought for a moment, then slapped her hand down on the counter. "I've got just the thing. Follow me." She led Jeremy over to a glass display case in the back that was filled with lockets.

"A heart-shaped locket? I don't know," Jeremy said dubiously.

The woman took a necklace out of the case and handed it to Jeremy. "Here. Look at this."

To his surprise, the tiny silver heart, hanging on a delicate silver chain, was actually a bottle. "It's an aromatic pendant," the woman explained. "They were very popular in Victorian times. Back then, women used to fill them with brandy, or another strong-smelling liquid, and sniffed them if they felt faint." She peered over her wire-rimmed glasses. "They're just perfect for filling with a favorite perfume or oil. And they come in a wide variety of sizes."

"Cool," Jeremy said, nodding. "I'll take it. But, uh, do you have any other shapes besides hearts?"

The woman smiled apologetically. "I'm afraid not." She checked her watch. "And we're closing in a few minutes. But if you come back later in the week, I might have a new shipment of the pendants in."

Jeremy frowned. A heart might send the wrong message. On the other hand, he didn't want to wait. "I—I guess I'll take that one, then," he said slowly, pointing to a small pendant inside the case.

"Excellent choice," the saleswoman said approvingly. "She's going to love it."

"I hope so," Jeremy said as she wrapped it up. He'd never bought a girl a present before. But this wasn't exactly a present. It was strictly a thank-you gift, he reminded himself.

Nothing more.

ELEVEN

"I'LL HAVE THE crab legs, please, with the wild-grain rice and a small Caesar salad." Liv closed her menu and handed it back to the server.

"And for you, Jeremy?" asked Mr. Clark.

"The landlubber entrée. The sixteen-ounce New York strip with peppercorn sauce and mashed potatoes, please." The Clarks knew he'd gotten sick last night. He suspected that they also knew he'd had a drink, but they didn't say anything about it. Jeremy was relieved. He was by no means a drinker, and if the Clarks had brought it up, he would have felt even more irresponsible and stupid than he already did. He knew that they trusted him and Patrick, and he didn't want to break that trust.

"The King Crab House is a landmark here in Beach Haven," Mrs. Clark said, taking a piece of warm corn bread from the bread basket. "We try to come here as often as we can during the summer. The food is excellent."

The restaurant sat on an inlet, on the other side of Ocean Parkway. Many of the summer residents kept their boats docked in one of the many slips that were available.

"I love the way they've got it set up," Liv remarked. It was a Victorian house that had been completely refurbished. Leather booths lined the glass-windowed wall and looked directly out onto the water. The middle of the room was filled with tables, and giant nets hung from the ceiling.

"It's nice," Jeremy said, smiling at her. She looked really pretty tonight. She wore a purple sarong, a snug-fitting white knit top, and matching sandals. Her hair was pulled back on the sides, making her cheekbones look even more pronounced. *Beauty, thy name is Liv.*

"Miss?" The server handed Liv, Mrs. Clark, and Patrick each a large plastic bib with a picture of a giant red crab on it.

"That's in case they spill all over themselves," informed Shelby from the seat beside Jeremy. "That's why I ordered the popcorn shrimp. Nice and neat."

Patrick laughed. "Hey, Liv. You could have used that bib earlier today, huh?"

Liv raised her eyebrows meaningfully. "Don't go there, Patrick."

Patrick took a bite of the salad that the server had just placed in front of him. "You wouldn't have believed what happened," he said to Shelby and his parents between mouthfuls. "Liv had been hanging out with the girls on the beach, right? But then she decided to come in and cool off, so Jeremy let her use his raft."

"Patrick," Liv warned again, giving him a pointed look.

"C'mon, don't be a baby! They'll think it's funny, Liv." He patted her arm. "So anyway, I'm watching her go out, right? And this killer wave comes along, and Liv and her raft catch it and come flying in on it. So then—"

"Does anyone want a fried zucchini stick?" Jeremy offered, holding up the basket. He could see that Liv was growing increasingly annoyed. *Is Patrick on another planet or what? Shut up already, yo-yo.* He couldn't stand to see her upset.

"I'll have one," Liv said, yanking one out.

"Like I was saying," Patrick continued, "Liv comes flying in on her raft. She stands up, all proud and all of how well she did, when Ben and Tim, you know, the Martin twins, go diving in the water next to her and come up yelling—"

At this point Patrick began to laugh uncontrollably. "There Liv stood, baring it all, I mean *all*, for the whole beach to see while the Martin twins played catch with her runaway bikini top."

"Cocktail sauce, anyone?" Jeremy asked desperately.

Mrs. Clark put down her fork. "I think that's enough, Patrick."

"I finally managed to get it away from them

while Liv clung to the raft like it was a life preserver or something," Patrick said between laughs. "Next time you better wear a one-piece when you're going on the raft."

Jeremy glanced at Liv. Her jaw was set. "I don't think I'll be going out rafting again anytime soon," she said curtly.

No one said anything for a few minutes.

"The Martin twins are such immature babies," Shelby said disdainfully, breaking the silence. "They constantly come up and splash me when I'm just getting in the water and run away. I hate them."

Patrick rubbed Liv's arm. "Hey, Liv, don't get bent out of shape or anything. It's pretty funny, you have to admit."

"Not to me, it wasn't." Liv dabbed at her mouth with her napkin.

"Face it, Patrick, you wouldn't like it if you lost your swim trunks out there in the middle of doing some awesome board move," Jeremy told him.

"This is the kind of thing I thought you'd find funny," Patrick said, turning to his friend. "When did you lose your sense of humor?"

"I just don't think making fun of someone, especially in front of other people, is very funny," Jeremy said quietly.

"Neither do I," Liv said. Just then the waiter hustled over, depositing his food-laden tray on a nearby cart.

"Crab legs!" he sang out.

★   ★   ★

"Liv, I think you're acting a little ridiculous here." Patrick put his arm around her.

She shrugged it off. "That's exactly the problem."

Patrick, Liv, and Jeremy were wedged in the backseat of the Camry. The food at the King Crab House had been great, but the bikini top mishap had cast a shadow over the meal.

"Quit moping, honey," Patrick said, tickling her in the ribs. "No one actually saw much. You dove for the raft too quickly."

Jeremy sighed. Didn't he see enough was enough? "Clark, drop it, okay? The nonjoke's over." It was like Patrick was going out of his way to make Liv mad. And he was doing an extremely good job of it.

Patrick grumbled something under his breath and leaned back. "You're making a mountain out of a—a molehill." He started to laugh. "Sorry, no pun intended there."

Even Jeremy had to crack a smile at that one.

Not Liv. In fact, when Jeremy laughed, she got even more annoyed looking than she'd been all night long. Her violet eyes looked at him as if to say, *You're making fun of me too?*

He couldn't win. He stood up for Liv, and Patrick got annoyed. And when he laughed at one of Patrick's jokes, Liv got annoyed.

Jeremy leaned forward. "So, Mr. Clark. How about those Pirates?"

It was late now, about eleven.

They'd all hung out in the family room for a

129

while playing gin rummy until Patrick got a phone call from one of his surfer buddies and had gone upstairs to take it. After he'd been gone for an hour, Liv had called it a night. Jeremy and Shelby devoured a pan of double fudge brownies and had played two killer games of Sony Playstation tennis before Mrs. Clark shuttled her off to bed.

Jeremy wondered what Liv was doing. To think that she was only yards away from him was so . . . so tempting. Spending the night in the same house with a girl you liked was a completely new experience for him. It felt strange. Intimate.

He thought of her after she closed her door at night, brushing her hair, changing into her pajamas, looking out the window onto the beach. Her every possible movement was being tracked inside Jeremy's brain. He couldn't stop thinking about her.

Was this how love felt? He didn't know. He'd never been in love before.

He went in the bathroom and brushed his teeth. Then he padded out to the hallway. He tapped lightly on Liv's door.

"Liv," he whispered. He could hear soft music playing inside. He waited. "Liv." He whispered louder. He hoped she was still awake.

The door opened. "Jeremy!" she said softly, her eyes wide.

"Hi. I'm going in the hot tub. Feel like joining me?" It was a risk, but he had to take it. He needed to talk to her in private.

Liv leaned against the doorway, her face a mixture

of expressions Jeremy couldn't read. "I don't think that would be a good idea—" she started.

"Please?" Jeremy touched her face with his fingertips and walked away.

He prayed she would come.

Five minutes later Liv slipped outside onto the deck, clad in a dark blue one-piece and a plush white terry cloth robe. Jeremy smiled to himself. *Yes!*

"Brrr! It got chilly out here." Liv shivered.

"It's the wind. It always makes it seem cooler than it is."

Steam was rising from the hot tub. "This feels so good," Jeremy said, positioning his back against one of the pulsating jets of gurgling water. "I'd love to have one of these at home after a day at school."

Liv slid down next to him. "These things make me completely sleepy. You'll have to make sure I don't doze off."

"You won't. Not when you're here with me." A small apologetic smile formed at the corners of his mouth. "Sorry you had a bad night."

"I didn't. I just got mad, that's all."

"Patrick can be a goof sometimes. He doesn't mean to hurt people; he just doesn't know when to stop."

Liv shrugged. "I'm over it. Really."

Jeremy's eyes twinkled. "I notice you're not wearing a bikini, though."

Liv laughed. "Touché."

Jeremy closed his eyes and sank a little deeper,

letting the water bubble over his shoulders. "Nice night, isn't it?"

"Yes."

"Liv?"

"What?"

Suddenly the thoughts he'd been thinking in private for days came spilling out. "I can't stop thinking about you, Liv. About us."

"Us? There is no us," she said flatly.

"But there could be," Jeremy pleaded. "There should be." Reaching over, he found her hand underneath the water. He clasped it gently, entwining her fingers with his. She didn't resist.

"Liv, please. I know we've only known each other for a short time, but I've never felt like this before."

"Stop it. You're scaring me." Liv turned her head, her hair blowing out behind her in the wind.

"I'm scaring myself." Jeremy reached over and turned her chin back so that she met his gaze. "Do you realize what I'm risking here?" he said, thinking out loud. "I'm propositioning my best friend's girlfriend. That's not me. I'm not the kind of guy who goes around raiding other guys' girls." His eyes locked on hers. "This isn't just some dumb crush, some summer fling. I—I think I might be in love with you, Liv. And I need to know how you feel. The truth. Not just what you think is the right thing to say."

Liv closed her eyes and leaned back against the railing that encircled the hot tub.

"If—if I'm out of line, Liv, and I very well may be, then I'm sorry. But I can't go on thinking we might have had a future together and I let it go without even trying."

A sudden gust of wind blew over them, making the chimes that hung nearby jingle. Still Liv didn't move.

Jeremy felt like a wounded, weak animal instead of the confident high-school senior he'd thought he was. If not for the whooshing of the hot tub, Jeremy was sure Liv would hear his heart beating.

"Have you even bothered to consider what this would do to Patrick?" Liv said in a low voice, opening her eyes. "You're causing problems, Jeremy. You're making me all confused. I—I don't want to discuss this anymore."

"Don't you think I'm driving myself nuts too?" Jeremy pleaded. "I don't want to hurt Patrick. He's my best friend. But ever since I met you, I . . ." He stared down into the swirling water. "You're all I think about, Liv," he said miserably. "And if you can tell me in all honesty that you're happy with Patrick, then I'll completely back off. But I—I don't think that's the case. Or else you wouldn't be here with me right now."

"Well, I am happy, Jeremy," Liv said thinly, shaking her fingers loose from his grasp. "Patrick is my boyfriend. You're not. End of story."

"But—"

"I didn't come here to hurt people or break promises."

Jeremy felt hot—not because of the hot tub, but because of shame. "I don't want to hurt anyone either. But I think we could be good together." He sighed. "I like you, Liv. I like you a lot—"

Suddenly the sliding glass doors crashed open.

"No fair! You didn't tell us you were having a midnight hot tub party!" Shelby shrieked, racing over and jumping in. Patrick was right behind her.

"I could hear the hot tub running from outside my window, and I knew it had to be you guys." Patrick's perfect white teeth chattered in the dark. "Shelby and I turned into raisins the first year we got it installed, but now we don't use it that much." He slid in up to his neck. "Feels good, huh?" He gave Liv a peck on the cheek.

"Yeah," she answered quietly. "It does."

"So tomorrow we're all on for Surf and Splash?" Patrick asked. They had decided to spend the day at the popular water park.

Jeremy nodded. "Sounds cool."

Shelby scowled. "I want to go too. You're so not fair, Patrick."

Patrick gave her a noogie. "Look, little pain, I've been there twice with you and your friends this summer, letting you do whatever you want, buying you way too much junk food and staying way too long. Now it's our turn."

"Aren't you going to be working on your sand castle for the big competition?" Liv prompted. "You were so excited about it at dinner."

"I guess I'll have to. But Patrick's still not being

fair." She stuck out her tongue at him. "Just because you want to be alone with Liv. I bet Jeremy wouldn't mind me coming."

"Uh-uh," Patrick said. "Jeremy has a date."

"You do?" Liv and Shelby asked in simultaneous shock.

"He does," Patrick said mysteriously.

"I, uh, do," Jeremy confirmed. He tried to smile. Patrick had told him as they'd dressed for dinner that he'd set him up with the perfect girl. What could he say? That he'd already found her?

"With who?" Liv asked, her eyes wide.

"Megan Pirelli." Patrick beamed. "I called her and asked her to go with us tomorrow. Isn't it perfect?"

Shelby sucked in her breath. "Ooh, she's nice."

"Megan," Liv said slowly. "Sure. Why not? They might be really *good together*."

Jeremy winced at the extra stress she put on the last two words. He glanced at her, a tiny smile of hope on his face. But all he got in return was a cold, hard, challenging stare.

Well, Liv could think whatever she wanted about his "date" with Megan. He'd told her the truth about how he felt. He'd laid it on the line.

Now it was up to her.

TWELVE

"THAT'LL BE $17.95," the black-lipsticked girl behind the counter said, giving her gum a loud snap.

Jeremy handed her a twenty-dollar bill and dutifully stuck out his arm. The girl slapped a neon green bracelet around his wrist. "Welcome to Surf and Splash. Enjoy."

It was a typical New Jersey August day: hot and humid. Jeremy walked over to where the others were standing, under the shade of an oak tree next to the park's locker bank.

"Here," Liv said, holding open one of the metal locker doors. "We've left some room for you." Jeremy took off his sandals and T-shirt and shoved them in. He had twenty dollars and change in his zippered swim trunks pocket along with a tube of lip balm. He should be fine with that. They'd all slathered on waterproof sun lotion when they'd left the house that morning.

"What do you guys want to go on first?" Patrick asked. "The water tubes get pretty crowded later on. They're cool."

"Want to do them now, then?" Liv suggested.

"Sounds good," Megan agreed. Jeremy nodded. He'd decided to make the best of a not-so-ideal situation. So he couldn't have Liv. So what? There were plenty of other girls at Beach Haven to meet. And he was with a really nice one now. He smiled at Megan.

"Let's do it," Jeremy declared, grinning.

They headed down a paved path to the left, Patrick and Liv hand in hand in the front and Jeremy and Megan bringing up the rear. Little signs in the shape of surfboards marked the distance: Wild Water Tubes . . . 0.04 Mile.

"Thanks a lot for inviting me," Megan told Jeremy as they walked together.

"It was Patrick's suggestion. Which I'm glad he made." He gave her a smile. She looked great in her one-piece white suit with a little metallic gold anchor on the chest. Her hair was slicked back behind her ears. True, she wasn't his type: He didn't usually go for blondes, and Megan was young, a sophomore. He liked a girl to be his age or older . . . a girl with more spirit and spunk. Sophisticated. Smart. Brunette. Someone like . . . He creased his forehead as if to shut out even the possibility of *her*. He wasn't going to think like that today.

Even if she was wearing a black bikini.

Even if she was walking only several feet away from him.

There was no use thinking about her. Because there she was, bikini and all, holding hands with Patrick.

"You know, I didn't get the chance to tell you yesterday, but I felt really bad that you got so sick the other night," Megan said, interrupting his thoughts.

"It wasn't your fault."

Megan made a wry face. "I was the one who got you that drink in the first place."

"Well, I was the one who drank it. I was stupid." Something he seemed to be making a habit of being lately.

She relaxed. "Anyway. I just wanted to say I'm sorry."

"Okay."

The line for the Wild Water Tube twisted its way up a large hill, making its way through fake palm trees and platforms looking out over the rest of the park. Luckily the line moved pretty quickly. When they reached the top, a skinny guy wearing a bright blue Surf and Splash polo shirt handed them each a bright blue foam core raft. "You two. Slide one," he instructed Patrick and Liv, motioning them to the right. "You two. Slide two."

"Yes, sir," Patrick intoned, giving the guy a mock salute.

Megan giggled and huddled next to Jeremy.

Patrick grabbed Liv's hand and flopped down on his raft. "Here we go!" he yelled, pushing off with his hands.

"Only one person on a mat!" the Surf and Splash guy called out. But Patrick and Liv had already slid off down the tube.

"That's Patrick for you," Jeremy confirmed to Megan. "My policy is ladies first." He stepped aside.

Megan stared into the giant tube. "Thanks, I guess."

"You think I'm being gallant, but I'm just chicken," he whispered confidentially.

Megan squeezed her eyes shut tight. "I'm going to do two things I never do. Headfirst and stomach down." She knelt on the mat as if she were praying and crossed herself. Then she lay down and shoved off. "Ahhh!" Her screams reverberated back through the tube.

Jeremy waited for the required ten seconds to lapse and then shoved off behind her in the same position. He yelped as the water sloshed over his body. It was freezing! The tube twisted and turned . . . it was kind of like being in a large intestine.

Before Jeremy could catch his breath, the tube opened up and he was dumped unceremoniously into the giant pool below.

He stood up, shaking the water from his eyes. "That was wild!"

A few feet away Megan stood up and sloshed over. She fell against him, laughing. "You should have seen the look on your face when you came out!" She started laughing again.

"No funnier than the look on your face when you went down," Jeremy said indignantly.

"Out of the pool, people. Keep it moving, keep it moving." A stern-faced woman on the side began to spray everyone who was still in the pool with icy cold water.

"Okay, okay, we're moving!" Jeremy yelped, slogging up the pool steps. He reached out and grabbed Megan's hand to help her.

Patrick and Liv were already out of the pool, waiting on the side. As Jeremy and Megan climbed out, laughing and shaking the water from their hair, Jeremy noticed Liv and Patrick staring at Megan, a curious expression on their faces. It was an expression he was personally quite familiar with after this week—but to see Liv and Patrick looking this way was a shock. *They're jealous,* Jeremy thought, astonished. *Seeing me have fun with Megan is making them jealous.*

He knew he was being juvenile, but he held on to Megan's hand a little longer than was necessary. This was what everyone wanted, wasn't it? Patrick wanted him to be set up with Megan, and Liv wanted him to leave her alone.

As they exited the tubes Jeremy could feel Liv's eyes on his back. *Now you know how it feels,* he thought. But he didn't feel particularly proud or happy.

Miserable was more like it.

★   ★   ★

By the time they'd finished lunch, the park was bulging at the seams. "There are way too many people here," Patrick complained, his eyes scanning the dripping crowd. "Too much flesh."

"Everybody had the same idea to stay cool that we did," Liv said. Seeing Megan and Jeremy having so much fun together made Liv feel kind of glum. *I'm happy they're happy, but . . .* Somehow things with Patrick just didn't seem the same as they'd been back home. There was a distance between them. As if they were only playing at being boyfriend and girlfriend.

Megan picked up a soggy park map someone had left behind on a nearby table. "We're right next to Old Man River. Want to try that next?"

"Sure," Patrick said. Liv and Jeremy nodded.

Old Man River was one of the tamer rides in the park. Giant inner tubes floated down a relatively peaceful waterway, ending up in a giant man-made lake. The ride was popular with couples.

"Jeez," Patrick said, shaking his head as they reached the entrance to the ride. "There's even a line for Old Man River." The little wooden sign in front of them said Wait from This Point: 15 Minutes.

"Well, we're here now," Liv answered, her arms folded in front of her chest. "Let's make the best of it."

The sun beat down on them as they inched their way toward the entrance to the ride.

A trickle of sweat slid down Jeremy's neck. "I think I'm going to forget about the inner tubes. I'm going to strip off my trunks and dive right in that water."

"Now that is something I'd like to get on film," Megan said, going to tap her waterproof camera. She gasped. "My camera! I must have left it on the table when we had lunch!"

Liv hesitated a moment before getting into the tube that was waiting. "We'll go back there when we're done here," she said, motioning for Patrick to join her. "Either someone took it or turned it in by now already."

"It's my mom's camera. She's going to kill me," Megan moaned.

"I'll go back and see if it's there," Patrick decided. "You guys go without me!"

"Patrick—" Liv started. Suddenly she didn't want to let him out of her sight.

Before she could finish, Patrick had pushed his way back through the line.

"Come on, come on, hurry up," said a harried-looking guy, motioning Megan and Jeremy with his hand. "We don't have all day here, folks." Four inner tubes, each holding a couple, bobbed along in the water together next to Liv, waiting for the guy to lift the gate and send them out.

Liv tried to scramble up from her inner tube. "But my boyfriend had to—"

"Looks like you're on your own," barked the guy, moving toward the gate.

"I'll go with her," Jeremy said immediately.

"No! I don't think that's a good idea!" Liv

exclaimed frustratedly. But Jeremy had already dropped into the tube next to Liv.

Megan hopped back a step. "I'll wait for Patrick."

"But—" Liv threw up her arms in defeat as the tubes began to move out into the waterway. "Whatever."

They floated along in silence for several minutes. The tubes floated down a winding river trail, cutting through trees and brush. And the "river" was warm . . . almost like bathwater.

"Ahhh. This is the life, isn't it?" Jeremy sighed, leaning back his head. He reached back and laid his left arm against the rubber behind Liv's head. She tried to ignore it.

"Look at them." Liv pointed up ahead, where some boys were spinning their tubes in circles, trying to bump into each other. They hooted with laughter.

Jeremy grinned. "That looks like Patrick and me six years ago. We had great times together."

Liv was silent. She felt like she should bring up what had happened last night in the hot tub. She'd been thinking about it for most of the afternoon. But after telling Jeremy off in no uncertain terms in her head, she suddenly felt shy. Confused. Like maybe she didn't want to tell him off after all.

She shivered.

"Hey. You've got goose bumps." Jeremy ran his finger across her leg. "Don't tell me you're cold. It's ninety degrees out here."

"Silly, isn't it?" Liv licked her lips. Her goose bumps had nothing to do with the weather. It was Jeremy. Jeremy. *Admit it. Just being near him makes you tingle.*

"Looks like you and Megan are having a good time together on your *date*," Liv said casually, allowing her hand to drag through the water.

"She's a great girl," Jeremy said thoughtfully. He shifted his body slightly, sending a ripple through the water. "Funny she doesn't have a boyfriend."

"She likes you," Liv said, regretting the words as soon as she'd said them. "It's so obvious."

Jeremy didn't say a word.

"I mean, Laura and Joyce told me she liked Patrick, but I think it's pretty apparent that she's changed her mind."

"Have you? Changed your mind?"

"About what?" Liv played dumb, running her hand along the rubber tubing.

"About us. I meant what I said last night, Liv. I really like you." His eyes twinkled. "I've tried not to, but it's not working."

"I—"

"Be honest with me. Please. Either we're just friends or we're more. And if we're more, we've got to tell Patrick."

"No way." She frowned. "Besides. You and Megan—"

Jeremy shook his head. "You're the one I like," he said softly. "I only like Megan as a friend. And I can't believe you're okay with pretending like

144

there's nothing between us when you know there is. You know."

Liv bit her lip. She did know. "This is really hard for me, Jeremy. I don't want to do something stupid."

"Then don't—"

Bam! They were slammed from behind. "Those kids . . ." Jeremy maneuvered the tube around.

"Hi!" It was Patrick and Megan, laughing and splashing their way over. "We broke the record for the fastest float down Old Man River," Patrick boasted.

"Got my camera too. Here. I'll take your picture." Megan giggled. "I guess I can't ask you guys to get closer. These tubes wedge you in like sardines."

Jeremy and Liv smiled self-consciously. "Now it's your turn," Jeremy said. Megan tossed him the camera. "Say Old Man River!"

Liv laughed as they mugged for the camera. But her insides were twisting at the sight of Patrick and Megan together. Laura and Joyce had been telling her the truth. Megan did like Patrick.

She'd felt indifferent when she heard the girls say it. But now, now that she saw them together . . .

Was she really ready to say good-bye?

Jeremy tossed and turned. He'd been lying in bed for at least an hour, and he didn't feel the least bit sleepy. He hated when this happened. Across the room the sound of Patrick's steady, even breathing was beginning to bug him. He thought briefly of waking him up so he'd have someone else to lie awake with.

He decided he might as well get up. Lying here listening to Patrick was only making things worse. Slipping out from underneath the covers, Jeremy pulled on a pair of sweatpants and a T-shirt and tip-toed out into the hallway.

The light over the kitchen stove was on, sending an eerie glow over the Clarks' kitchen. Jeremy opened the refrigerator and peered inside.

Ham, Swiss cheese, and green-leaf lettuce. Perfect. His mouth began to water as he spread a thick layer of mayonnaise on some rye bread he'd found in the bread bin. Oops. Almost forgot the tomato. He rummaged through the refrigerator again. No tomato.

He slumped against the counter. He felt like the guy in that old mayonnaise commercial. A sandwich just wasn't a sandwich without a slice of thick, ruby red tomato.

"Looking for one of these?"

Startled, Jeremy dropped the package of cheese slices on the floor. It was Liv, barefoot, dressed in cutoffs and a gray sweatshirt. In her hand was a tomato.

"How'd you guess? And where was it?"

She pointed to the windowsill in the hallway. "Mrs. Clark puts the ones that still need to ripen there to catch some sunshine. She says if you put them in the refrigerator, they lose their taste."

"Oh. Well, thanks." Jeremy caught the tomato as Liv tossed it and bent to pick up the cheese. "Can I make you something?"

Liv examined Jeremy's sandwich critically. "Make me one too. Smaller, though." She opened the refrigerator. "Milk?"

"Yeah."

She poured two tall glasses full. "Couldn't sleep, huh?"

"Nope." He sliced the tomato. "You either?"

"No." Liv unlocked the bolt on the sliding glass doors and grabbed the milk glasses. "Let's eat outside."

They wiped off their chairs with a beach towel that was hanging to dry on the deck and sat down. It was a nice night. Not as humid and muggy as it had been earlier in the day. The ocean breeze felt cool and refreshing.

Jeremy bit into his sandwich. For some reason food always seemed to taste better late at night. Maybe it was the whole comfort factor.

"We need to talk," Liv said, clearing her throat after they had finished eating.

"*You* want to talk?" Jeremy quipped.

Liv flung a crumb at him. "Don't play games, Jeremy."

"*You* talk, then. You know exactly where I stand."

Liv started to speak, then clamped her mouth shut. "Can we go for a walk or something?" She glanced up at the house, shrouded in the shadows.

"I feel uncomfortable talking about this here." She started to gather up the plates.

"Leave them. We'll get them on the way back. Come on." Wordlessly Liv stood up. They walked down the steps and onto the deserted beach.

THIRTEEN

THE WHITE WOODEN lifeguard chair, barely noticeable during the day when the beach was crowded with umbrellas and people, stood out like a giant white jack-in-the-box at night.

"Do you want to go up there and sit for a while?" Jeremy asked after they'd walked for about half a mile. "No one will see us," he added.

"Oh, that's great," Liv said under her breath. "'No one will see us.' What kind of statement is that?"

"You know what I meant, Liv," he answered forlornly. "I don't want people to get the wrong . . . impression."

"Kind of hard to do that, I suppose," Liv said as she hoisted herself up in the chair. "A guy and a girl on the beach at midnight, cuddled up in the lifeguard chair together?" She sat down. "If it looks like a fish and smells like a fish . . ."

They were silent for a while.

"I can remember visiting Virginia Beach with my mom and Andrea when I was twelve," Liv said suddenly. "We stayed at this hotel right on the beach, and our room looked out over the pool. We'd go swimming and hang out on the beach all day long, just the three of us. And at night my mom and Andrea would sit out on the balcony, listening to the ocean and talking to each other. But me, I'd grab a beach towel and go sit below on the sand with my Walkman on."

She looked at Jeremy. "I'd watch the couples walking by, and first I'd wish it was my mom and dad, happy together. But I knew it wasn't. And then I'd wish it were me, that I was old enough to have a boyfriend and feel as happy as they looked."

"But that was when you were a kid, Liv. It's different now."

Jeremy took her hand. He thought of the heart pendant. The necklace was inside his suitcase in Patrick's room. He'd tried to tell himself it was just a thank-you gift. But that wasn't true. It was a gift from the heart. And Jeremy couldn't give Liv a gift like that if she was still Patrick's girlfriend.

"No, it's not. Because I still feel that way when I'm with Patrick. Like, lately I'm waiting for the happy feelings to kick in." Tears welled up in her eyes. "That's not how you feel with a boyfriend." She shook her head, big tears spilling from her eyes.

"You're being too hard on yourself, Liv," Jeremy said quietly.

"But Patrick deserves a girlfriend who's honest and trustworthy." Liv laughed bitterly. "Characteristics that used to apply to me. I *thought* I wanted a commitment with him, but now . . ."

Jeremy squeezed her hand. The waves crashed against the beach, their foam dancing along the shore.

"Now there's you," she whispered. "And I don't know what I think anymore."

They sat there, holding hands and not speaking, for a long time.

"I'm going to break up with him, Jeremy," Liv said suddenly. "I have to." The tears came then, rushing and heavy. Jeremy inhaled sharply. He'd wanted to have a chance with Liv more than anything, but the idea of her actually breaking up with Patrick frightened him.

"Are you sure?"

"I can't keep things how they are. It's not right."

Without thinking, Jeremy took Liv's face in his hands. "I think I love you, Liv," he blurted out impulsively.

Liv swallowed. "I think I—"

Jeremy kissed her. All that mattered was his lips on her neck, his hands in her hair, her breath in her ear.

He and Liv were together.

And they would have to tell Patrick.

But how?

Liv snapped the blinds shut. She piled the pillows that littered the bed on the chair and turned down the bedcovers, smoothing them. She folded her sweater and hung her jeans up in the armoire. Quietly she held her sandals over the garbage can and brushed away the sand that remained.

Everything was in order. Neat and tidy, just like she liked things.

Everything, that was, except her life.

Liv's mind was a blur as she pulled her comfortable old T-shirt over her head. Jeremy's face kept coming into her mind, his eyes, so warm and adoring, his words, like silk, caressing her ears. No boy had ever made her feel like that before. Corny, maybe. But true.

Then her thoughts drifted to Patrick. Patrick asking for her phone number back in May. Their first date: A movie she couldn't even remember because she was too busy concentrating on the feel of his warm hand in hers. Skipping her junior prom and driving to the lake instead for a twilight picnic. Meeting Mr. and Mrs. Clark and Shelby for the first time, and the way they made her feel really welcome in their home.

For the second time that night a tear trickled down her cheek. *What am I supposed to do?* She felt like calling her mom, but there was no way she could tell her everything over the phone. Life had gotten so complicated in a few short days.

Was it possible to be in love with two guys at once? The feelings Liv had for Patrick were real, she knew that. And the times they'd shared were really special to her. Yet she couldn't deny that she had feelings for Jeremy too. If she felt this much for a guy she'd only known a few days, did that mean she was supposed to be with him?

The idea of breaking up with Patrick made her sick.

The idea of never seeing Jeremy again made her even sicker.

It was a no-win situation.

A light rap on the door startled her. Quickly she dried her eyes and blew her nose. Jeremy had to stop this. They were going to get caught. They couldn't keep meeting in secret. It was wrong.

She opened the door. "You've got to st—"

"Hello, gorgeous." Patrick moved inside and carefully closed the door. It didn't make a sound.

"Patrick—"

"Shhh." He wrapped his arms around her. "You've been here five nights already, and we haven't had one midnight rendezvous. What's the matter with us?" He sniffed Liv's hair. "You smell like the sea."

She forced herself to laugh. "I do?" She gestured to the hallway. "This probably isn't a good idea. What if your parents—"

"My parents are sound asleep. Besides, their air conditioner is so loud, they wouldn't hear a party going on downstairs." He grinned. A shock of blond hair spilled over his forehead.

"Okay." Liv shivered in her oversize T-shirt. But it wasn't from the temperature in the room.

This was turning into a nightmare.

Patrick walked over and opened the blinds.

"You've got yourself barricaded up in here. Look outside. Isn't it gorgeous tonight? Perfect for a midnight walk."

Liv's palms were moist. "Yeah, I guess it is." She desperately wanted him to leave. If he didn't, she didn't know what totally horrible thing she might do or say. She didn't want to tell him now. She needed time to think, to plan what she was going to say.

"Come over here." He motioned to her.

Liv walked over slowly, a bit unsteadily. "Patrick, I—"

"No talking. We've talked too much lately. All I want to do is kiss you."

His lips touched her forehead, trailing down her nose to rest on her mouth. He kissed her firmly, long and slow. Liv found herself kissing him back. Patrick tasted familiar . . . like Colgate and Chap Stick. His hair brushed her face, all soft and freshly shampooed.

"I've wanted to do this all day," he whispered, pulling her close.

"Me—me too," Liv whispered back, all at once meaning it and not meaning it, and hating herself for not knowing which it was.

Patrick pulled Liv down into the lumpy green chair, wrapping his arms around her. "Are you having a good time at Beach Haven?" he asked, his breath warm in her ear.

"Of course I am," she whispered, her back to him. She curled up in his arms. "It's a wonderful place. Now I know why you love it so much."

Patrick murmured something unintelligible in her ear.

"We'll be going back to school soon," she said softly. "To Erie, and—"

"Shhh. Don't spoil the mood." Patrick leaned over and began to kiss her again, more intently than he had the first time. She felt stiff, tense, unable to enjoy Patrick's soft, familiar kisses. Then a horrible thought raced into her mind.

Jeremy was lying alone in the next room.

He knew where Patrick was. And what he was doing. What *they* were doing.

The thought filled her with anxiety and fear. Breathlessly she scrambled to her feet.

"I—I've had enough for tonight. You should go." Her voice sounded quaky even to her own ears. "We've had a long day."

"What's the matter?" Patrick asked, his voice full of hurt. "You used to love kissing me. Lately I don't know—I feel like you're pushing me away."

Liv turned around to face him. His eyes were puzzled and concerned, filling her with an inexplicable pain. "I'm not pushing you away, Patrick," she said softly. "I just feel tired, that's all. And I don't feel right, making out in here. It's like we're hiding from your parents or something."

Patrick sighed. "You don't like me to touch you when we're around other people and you don't like kissing when we're alone. You're a hard girl to figure out, Olivia Carlson."

"I'm still trying to figure me out myself."

Patrick gave her one more kiss, this time on her cheek. "Well, when you do, I'll be right next door waiting for you, okay?"

She smiled tiredly. "Okay."

"Sleep good, then." Patrick gave her a small wave and tiptoed into the hall, shutting the door behind him.

"'Night."

Liv sagged against the door.

What was she doing? She'd thought she'd known for sure that it was Jeremy she wanted when they were outside on the chair. She'd even been going over what to say to Patrick, how to break the news to him gently. She didn't want to hurt him. Ever. But after seeing Patrick, after kissing him once more, after thinking about what they'd shared, she was more confused than ever. How had her feelings for her boyfriend changed? Had they changed enough to make her give him up forever?

Liv flung herself down on the bed, hiding her face in the fluffy pillows as the tears began to fall for the third time that night in a silent, steady stream. She caught one with her tongue and swallowed, the salty wetness tickling her throat.

But it didn't do what she'd hoped it would. She still had the horrible bitter taste on her chapped lips and in her stomach.

The taste of betrayal.

FOURTEEN

"C'MON. LET'S GO outside," Jeremy suggested. He felt like he was going to jump out of his skin from the tension in the house. He and Liv had been staring at each other across the kitchen table since Mrs. Clark had left to go grocery shopping. Patrick had been gone since early morning. He had promised to help his dad out down at the marina for a few hours. Liv had offered to watch Shelby, who was outside on the beach.

They walked out on the deck. Several hundred feet in front of the house people were busy shoveling sand into buckets and sand molds. Jeremy glimpsed Shelby's long ponytail and bright red bathing suit. She was giving instructions to two shorter-looking boys.

"The Martin twins," Liv and Jeremy said at the same time, laughing. He felt the tension ease.

"I guess you haven't talked with Patrick yet,"

Jeremy said, leaning against the railing. Dumb comment. When Patrick found out, Jeremy would definitely know.

Liv shook her head. "No. Not exactly. It's not something I can just *do*, you know?"

Jeremy nodded. "I've been trying to think what I'm going to say myself. 'By the way, Patrick, I'm in love with your girlfriend'?" He shook his head. "Nope. Doesn't quite work."

The sun poured down on them. Liv's eyes started to water. "Do you mind if we don't talk about this right now? I kind of want to go chill out on the beach for a while."

Jeremy watched her walk into the house.

When she came back out, she had changed from the shorts and T-shirt she'd had on to a purple bikini. She handed Jeremy a bottle of Coppertone.

"Would you mind putting this on my back? I don't want to get burned."

"Sure," Jeremy said. There was nothing he'd like to do more. Liv lifted her hair off her shoulders and neck.

Slowly Jeremy began to massage the lotion into her back, making sure not an inch of her lovely skin went unprotected. Her body felt warm and pliable, and his hands rubbed the lotion into her shoulder blades, her arms, her lower back.

Liv's posture grew relaxed, and she began to sway slightly under his touch.

Instinctively Jeremy leaned forward. He pressed his lips softly against the back of Liv's neck.

"Liv," he whispered, covering her neck and shoulders with tiny kisses. "Do you know how much I—I—"

"You what?" Liv asked, turning to face him. She let her hair go, letting it fall softly around her face.

Jeremy's heart was in his mouth. He didn't think he'd ever seen anyone more beautiful than Liv was at that moment. Without speaking, he wrapped his arms tightly around her. "This," he murmured, leaning forward and gently placing his lips against hers.

This kiss was different than the others they'd shared. It was soft and sweet and knowing. Liv hadn't said she loved him, but her lips told him all he needed to know. She felt the same way he did. They were meant to be together. . . .

"Yo, guys, it's just me. My dad told me ten times not to forget the Dirt Devil for the boat, and wouldn't you know—" Patrick stopped at the doorway to the deck, his mouth hanging open. "What the hell—"

Jeremy felt as if the wind had been knocked out of him. *Patrick!* Jeremy stood there, motionless. He couldn't move. He couldn't think.

He watched in horror as Liv stumbled away from him. "Patrick," she whispered. "It's not what you think."

Liv touched his shoulder. Patrick angrily swatted her hand away. "You backstabbing phony!" he shouted, lunging for Jeremy. He knocked him squarely on the jaw—an easy feat, considering

159

Jeremy was frozen in place. Jeremy fell back into a deck chair. He didn't even feel the impact. He was numb.

"Not what I think?" Patrick's voice sounded like it belonged to someone else. His eyes shot daggers at Jeremy. "Think? I think my *best friend* is a lying, cheating scumbag."

Jeremy touched his jaw. He tasted blood. This was exactly what he'd feared. He could barely look at Patrick. *This isn't real. This can't be happening.*

Patrick slammed his fist against the wall. One of Mrs. Clark's watercolors crashed to the floor. "Making out with my girlfriend when I step out of the house for two minutes!"

"Patrick, please," Liv pleaded, tears streaming down her face. She reached out for his shoulder again. "You've got to listen to me. It's not Jeremy's fault. I—"

Patrick glared at her, his eyes wild. "Don't touch me," he said, shaking. "This is real nice, Liv. No wonder you guys were so happy to stay here while I was away. Sorry I came back and spoiled your afternoon."

"Patrick—" Jeremy started.

"Shut up." Patrick's voice was low and gravelly. "Don't you say a word. I want both of you out of here when I come back. Go get a motel room or something. Just—just get out of here."

Jeremy felt as if he was about to pass out. "Please, Patrick. Just calm down. We can—we can . . ."

Liv stood rooted to the deck, sobbing quietly.

Patrick backed up, his face a mixture of hurt and anger. "I can't believe this. Jeremy, you . . . I thought we were friends."

He took off back through the house. Jeremy ran after him, his heart racing. "Wait, Patrick. Give me a chance to explain."

Patrick spun around when he reached the front door. "A friend shouldn't have to explain a scene like that. Ever."

The wooden door slammed shut in Jeremy's face.

He stood there for a moment, trying to collect his thoughts. Then he walked back out to the deck. Liv was slumped down in a lounge chair, taking deep, raspy breaths of air.

Jeremy panicked. "You're not hyperventilating, are you?"

Liv shook her head emphatically. She stood up, holding on to the chair for support. "I can't believe what just happened. Patrick knows," she whispered. She let out a little gasp.

"It was an accident," Jeremy cried, trying to comfort her. "He wouldn't listen to me—"

"Accident?" Liv sputtered, wiping her nose. "The only accident was me ever getting involved with you in the first place!"

"Liv, wait—" Jeremy said. He put his arms around her, but she angrily shoved him away.

"No, you wait. If you would have *waited,* this never would have happened! Patrick's the nicest guy I've ever dated. And I've totally screwed up everything!" Liv ran inside and shoved her feet into her sandals. Jeremy ran after her. "You've got to let me borrow your car. I've got to stop him." She was sobbing again by this point. "Please, Jeremy."

Jeremy didn't know what to do. Liv was way too upset to drive. And he didn't think running after Patrick was a good idea anyway. At least not now. "I don't think you should do that," he said. "Let him cool off. We'll talk to him later."

"Please, Jeremy," she sobbed. "I need to go now."

"Then let me come with you," he pressed.

"No!" she burst out, crying even harder. "I need to be alone with him."

This made Jeremy wince. "Okay," he said finally. "Listen to me. Take a few deep breaths. You're in no shape to drive."

She nodded, her chest heaving. "Okay."

Then, feeling too weak to stop her, Jeremy took his keys out of his pocket and dropped them in Liv's outstretched palm.

"I'm fine." She gulped. "Just wait for me here, okay? Don't leave. He didn't mean it." She turned and fled the room.

But Jeremy knew she was wrong. Patrick did mean it. His best friend had caught him with his girlfriend.

Eight years of being like brothers didn't matter when it came to love.

His friendship with Patrick was over.

FIFTEEN

LIV HEADED STRAIGHT for the marina. Adrenaline pumped through her veins. In a few minutes she spotted Patrick, hunched over his bike, pedaling like a madman.

"Patrick," she called, rolling down the passenger window. "Patrick!"

He didn't turn around.

"Please, Patrick," she sobbed, driving the car half on the road, half on the shoulder. Behind her a driver honked his horn.

She ignored it. Liv tried to call Patrick's name again, but she couldn't get the words out. By now she was crying so hard that she was afraid she might have an accident if she didn't pull over.

Shaking, she parked the car on the side of the road and got out. By now Patrick was a good block away from her.

Liv stood there, trembling. "Nice body!"

screamed a bunch of guys in a passing Jeep. For the first time Liv realized all she had on was the bikini. But she didn't even care. She began to walk unsteadily down the road.

After a few blocks she saw that she was gaining. *How can that be?* she wondered. Then she realized that Patrick had stopped too. As she got closer she saw that he had gotten off his bike and was sitting on a concrete bench.

She sat down beside him. "I'm sorry."

His head was in his hands. "Sorry?"

"Yes, I'm . . . I'm sorry, Patrick." She longed to reach out and hold him, to tell him what he'd seen was a lie. That they'd never meant to hurt anyone, least of all him.

Patrick lifted his eyes to meet hers. "How could you? How could you do that to me?"

She struggled to find the right words. "I wasn't . . . doing it to you. We . . . we just had some kind of connection."

"You and Jeremy." Patrick laughed. "This is some kind of bad dream. You and Jeremy have a connection."

"I know it sounds—"

"It sounds like a bunch of crap!" Patrick screamed. "What about our connection, huh? What about our boyfriend-girlfriend connection? Or did that slip your mind?"

Liv flinched as if she'd been slapped. Her heart was about to pound right out of her chest. She'd sort of pictured what breaking up might be like, but this was much, much worse than she'd imagined.

And now that it was actually happening, she realized she didn't want it to. At least not yet.

"Jeremy and I made a mistake," Liv said numbly.

"When? When did this start?"

"Last Saturday. When we got stuck in the woods . . ." The words were sticking in her throat and she felt dull-witted, like she couldn't put a coherent sentence together if she tried.

Patrick nodded. "How convenient. And you've been making a fool of me all week long. Thanks, Liv. Thanks a lot." He stood up and stalked away. "What an idiot I've been."

"Patrick, wait." Liv ran up behind him. "Neither one of us planned for this to happen. It just . . . you kept telling me what a great guy he was, right?" she prompted, forcing herself to smile. She wrung her hands together. "Well, he is. And I—I've fallen for both of you. Please, Patrick," she cried as he stomped toward his bike. "Don't be like this. Don't let my mistake erase what we have together. Isn't what we have worth something? Don't just throw it away."

Patrick looked back at Liv. "You threw it away the moment you kissed Jeremy. You gave up on us." For the first time since it happened, his voice sounded seminormal.

Weakly Liv sat down on the grass. "I'm not giving up on you now," she said, her voice barely above a whisper.

She caught her breath as he sat down beside her.

"Hold me, Liv," he said, a tear sliding down his cheek.

And she did.

Jeremy whistled a Smashing Pumpkins song and tried to look on the bright side. Which was kind of hard to do at the moment. Especially with his jaw feeling like he'd rammed it into a concrete wall.

He'd been walking the beach for three hours . . . past the pier and now back. He'd never seen Patrick so mad in his life. Never. Not when Patrick got detention, not when he got in a fight with that jerk Billy Crawford, not even when he broke his arm and had to sit out a whole rugby season.

The fact that Patrick might hate him scared Jeremy. Terrified him. He'd have no one to talk to. To . . . trust. *Should have thought about that a week ago, loser.*

Jeremy checked his watch. What was going on right now? Was Liv breaking it to him gently? Was Patrick even bothering to listen? Were they making a scene on Ocean Parkway? He sighed. This vacation was definitely not turning out as he'd planned.

Suddenly Jeremy remembered he was supposed to be watching Shelby. He'd forgotten all about her. "You are such an idiot, Thomas," he muttered, jogging back up the crowded beach.

To his relief, he spotted Shelby right away. She was patting the side of a giant lion. "Hey, Shelby," he panted, jogging up.

"Hi!"

At least someone was glad to see him. "What do we have here?"

"The Sphinx," said a brown-haired, freckle-faced boy beside him. "We decided making a regular sand castle was too boring for the contest."

"Hmmm. You guys are pretty smart. What do you get if you win?"

Shelby scratched her head. "Some gift certificates from the beach shops and stuff. It's more about the competition than the prizes."

"Oh."

Shelby stared at Jeremy. "What's wrong with your cheek? It's all puffy."

"Nothing. I just had a little accident."

"You look sad." She scrunched up her mouth. "Is this about you and Liv?"

Kids. Jeremy stepped teasingly on her toe, making her squeal. "What do you know about me and Liv?"

Shelby crossed her arms. "I know that you like her. I can tell."

Jeremy smiled. "Like I said, you're pretty smart."

"They've been up there for a while now." Shelby pointed to the deck of Pelican's Cove.

"Up there . . ." Jeremy trailed off. Patrick and Liv were up on the deck. "We'll talk later, Shelb. Okay?"

"Okay. Good luck."

Jeremy smiled. "Thanks."

The walk up to the deck seemed to last forever. As he climbed the steps Jeremy waited for Patrick to come over and throw him off. But he didn't.

Patrick and Liv were sitting outside, glasses of iced tea in front of them. Liv's hair was wet, pulled back in a loose ponytail. She had changed into jeans and a T-shirt. Next to their feet was a pile of corn on the cob, a large metal bowl, and a bag of husks.

"Hi," Jeremy said. *Don't be so nervous!*

"Hi," Liv answered. Patrick took a sip of iced tea.

"So." Jeremy jammed his hands in his pockets. The silence was excruciating. "Did you guys, uh, talk?" he asked awkwardly.

Liv nodded. "Uh-huh." Jeremy pulled out a chair and sat down. "We had a pretty long talk."

Jeremy glanced over at Patrick. He stared straight ahead, stone-faced and silent. *He's taking this better than I thought he would. At least he's sitting here with us both.*

"We decided that things had moved a little too fast." Liv bit her lip. "We kind of resolved things."

Jeremy nodded encouragingly. This was going better than he'd expected. "Well, uh, good. I'm glad. I mean, we can't all go around hating each other, you know?" He tried to smile. "I know you're really angry with me, Patrick, but I appreciate your being so cool right now. I'm sure Liv does too."

He reached over to pat Liv on the knee. She shook her head imperceptibly. "No, Jeremy." She hesitated. "You don't understand. I—I'm not going to end things. I mean, we're not going to."

Patrick bent down, grabbed an ear of corn, and began to shuck.

"I'm not sure I'm following you," Jeremy said slowly, looking from Liv to Patrick as if he were watching a tennis match.

"What she's saying is that despite your attempts, we're still a couple," Patrick said coldly. He tossed the husks in the bag and picked up another ear. "I'm not breaking up with her. And she's not breaking up with me."

Jeremy pushed his chair back from the table. "You're not?" he said, staring at Liv. He couldn't believe this.

"No." Patrick's eyes locked with Jeremy's until Jeremy had to look away.

"We had a long talk, Jeremy," Liv explained, her eyes downcast. "I realized that I hadn't really thought things through. Patrick and me—our relationship—means a lot," Liv said. Her voice shook. "And I'm not ready to give it up. Patrick's willing to forgive me." Patrick took her hand. "I—I'm sorry."

Jeremy was dumbfounded. He'd run through a million scenarios in his head as he walked the beach, but this wasn't one of them. Liv was staying with Patrick. They weren't breaking up.

"There's no need to apologize," Jeremy said, trying to contain the bitterness that filled his heart. "I can handle it." But inside he was crestfallen. How could Liv do this? Sure, Liv was Patrick's girlfriend, but after all they'd shared together? After their kiss today? *Didn't that mean anything to her?*

"I'm going to go in the house," Liv said suddenly,

standing up. She brushed the corn silk from her jeans. "Sorry it had to be this way," she mumbled, her eyes darting quickly to Jeremy. Then she turned and ran inside.

The bright red berry slices fell neatly into the bowl. Liv was eager to do anything to help Mrs. Clark with dinner. Anything to take her mind off the awful scene of earlier that afternoon.

"Is everything all right, Liv?" Mrs. Clark asked, checking on the chicken cutlets she had baking in the oven. "Everyone seems so down in the mouth around here."

"We kind of had a . . . a misunderstanding today. All of us." She stared into the bowl of strawberries. She couldn't bear to tell Mrs. Clark what had happened. She'd find out sooner or later. Let it be later. Liv couldn't take much more today.

"I'm sure it's nothing that strawberry shortcake and whip cream won't fix," Mrs. Clark said, grinning. "Oops. There's the phone. Hello? Oh, hi, Nancy . . ."

Liv wished that were the case. She'd make enough for fifty people if it was.

Suddenly the glass door opened and Patrick strode in the room. "Hi," Liv said, her voice hopeful. "Get enough sun out there?" she attempted to joke.

Patrick came over and popped a berry in his mouth. "Just so you know. Jeremy's not going to be staying here anymore."

Liv dropped her knife on the counter. "You mean not in your room, right? You've asked him to sleep in the den or—"

"No. He's not staying here. Am I not speaking in plain English?" Patrick's voice was as cold as ice. "He's going to sleep out in the loft in the garage."

"Patrick, no. That's not right. You can't do that." Liv was mortified at the thought.

"I can and I did." He gave her a fixed look. "You should be grateful. My first instinct was to kick his butt out of here completely." He paused. "But he *was* my best friend. I can't be that heartless." He grabbed another berry and walked out of the room.

Liv squeezed her eyes half shut and tried to keep the tears from falling. Patrick and Jeremy's friendship was ruined, and it was all because of her. She squeezed her eyes tighter.

Didn't work.

SIXTEEN

"**L**OOKS LIKE IT'S going to rain."

Liv followed Patrick's gaze upward. Dark, heavy clouds were beginning to crowd each other out in the early afternoon sky.

"So you aren't wasting a good beach day after all," Liv said as they headed inside the Riverhaven Mall.

Patrick sighed as he held open the door. "When was spending time with each other ever a waste?"

They'd been trying to be a couple again for the past several days. But it was hard. Liv knew Patrick was still resentful of Jeremy. And she couldn't blame him—even though it was breaking her heart to see Jeremy suffer like he so obviously was.

Liv steered Patrick into the junior department at Macy's. Big back-to-school signs were hung from the ceiling, and TVs in the walls blasted rock videos.

"Are you looking for anything in particular?" a clerk asked, coming up to them.

Liv shook her head. "Just looking." She fingered a velvet short-sleeved mock turtleneck.

"You'd look nice in that," Patrick offered.

Liv hung the hanger back on the rack. "You think?"

Patrick nodded.

Liv stared down at the floor. Here they were, trying to be a couple again when they both knew it could never be like before. She hated the awkward feeling that sat in the pit of her stomach. She'd never felt this way around Patrick. They used to just have fun together. Now it was just one heavy-duty guilt trip.

"Do you want to go in the Record Bin? Check out the new releases?" Patrick suggested.

"Okay." *I wonder what Jeremy's doing.*

Once inside, Patrick put on a pair of headphones and listened to some new alternative release while Liv flipped halfheartedly through the latest dance stuff.

It wasn't any different in the bookstore. Patrick headed for the boarding magazines while Liv pored over the latest fashion magazines.

Spending the day together? *Not.*

As they headed down one of Riverhaven's huge corridors Liv noticed a guy and a girl standing near the mall's water fountain. The girl was wearing a shirt from the Gap that Liv had at home in her closet. The guy had his arms around the girl's waist, and she was smiling up at him, her head tilted to the side. They were completely wrapped up in each other. When the girl leaned forward and kissed him, Liv smiled.

"What?" Patrick asked, noticing her expression.

"Oh, nothing. Them, I guess." Liv nodded in the couple's direction. "They look happy. It made me happy. Silly, huh?"

"Nothing you do is silly," Patrick said. To Liv's surprise, he slipped his arm around her. He hadn't shown her much affection since their almost breakup. "We could try to be like that again, Liv."

Liv looked into Patrick's eyes. "Try?" she repeated softly. "We never had to try before."

Patrick looked at her for a few seconds in silence. "I guess you're right." He started walking down the corridor. Liv hurried to catch up.

"Don't, Patrick," Liv urged. "Can't we be honest with each other?" Patrick chuckled. "I mean—" Liv faltered, trying to find the right words to say. "Isn't that what we *are* doing here? Trying to give our relationship another chance?" She smiled brightly at him. "Frozen yogurt. My treat."

Patrick took Liv's hand, and as they walked toward the food court he gave her fingers a little squeeze, just like he always did.

Liv squeezed his fingers back tightly.

She wasn't ready to let go.

"How—how can you even talk to me?" Liv mumbled as she and Mrs. Clark finished drying the dinner dishes Thursday night. She hadn't been able to look Patrick's mother in the eye since Shelby had told the Clarks everything on Sunday. Liv hadn't even been there for dinner, but she needed to keep busy.

After leaving the mall, she and Patrick had driven to a pretty café up the coast for dinner and stopped at a few souvenir shops. They'd even hit the art museum.

But the day hadn't been fun. Oh, sure, they'd maintained upbeat fronts. Patrick had bought a new shirt, Liv got some souvenir postcards and boxes of saltwater taffy for her friends, and they'd both proclaimed dinner was "fab." *But you're just a big fat liar, Liv Carlson, and you know it.* She was too busy feeling guilty and sad to enjoy anything, and Patrick, although he denied it, was totally mistrustful. Could she blame him? The magic that had once been there between them was gone. Liv knew it, and, she suspected, so did Patrick. But she had promised to try and work things out, and that was a promise she wasn't about to break.

Liv picked up a plate and began to rub her dish towel across it. "I've made a total mess of everything," she confessed. "And I've been pretty horrible to Patrick." Liv's lower lip began to tremble. "I feel so ashamed." Her voice was barely audible. She began to cry.

Mrs. Clark smoothed a lock of hair off Liv's forehead. "Liv, I love both of these boys. Patrick's my son, and Jeremy is just like a son . . . he's been a part of our family for so many years, I sometimes forget I didn't give birth to him."

Liv managed to smile.

"And believe me, I'd stand between them and anyone who I thought wanted to do them harm." She led Liv over to the kitchen table and poured them each a steaming cup of coffee. "Maternal instinct, you know. But that's not what you're trying to do, Liv. You've been caught up in the classic romantic problem that's been plaguing people for centuries: a love triangle."

"But I never wanted this to happen," Liv pleaded. "You've got to believe me."

"Of course I do." She leaned over and patted Liv's knee. "Don't be so tough on yourself. You've only just started to navigate down the rocky road of love. How can you be expected to make the right decisions at every corner?"

"I just want to be happy," Liv said, her voice small and thin.

"Everyone wants to be happy. But remember, happiness isn't a right, Liv. It's a privilege. And you've been fortunate enough to find happiness with two wonderful guys, and you're barely sixteen." She smiled. "Some girls never find it."

"They're the lucky ones," Liv mumbled, cradling the warm mug in her hands.

"Liv, honey, I can't tell you if Patrick's the boy for you. Only you know what's in your heart. You've got to do what will make you feel happy." She clasped Liv's hands inside her own. "Love is never easy."

*   *   *

"And Thomas goes for the rebound!" Jeremy grabbed the ball and shot it cleanly through the hoop. "Another amazing basket." He stopped to wipe the sweat from his brow. He'd been shooting hoops in the Clarks' basketball court for the past hour or two. Anything to get his mind off Liv.

He moved the ball around the court—behind his back, under his legs, out and in. Then he dribbled over and got in position for a few free throws. *Whish.* Perfect rotation. The first shot slid easily through the net. As did the second. And the third. He was on fire. Why couldn't this happen when he was in a real game?

As Jeremy lined up to take another shot Patrick jogged out into the driveway.

Jeremy gathered his courage. "Want to shoot some hoops, Clark?"

"Can't." Patrick unlocked the door to the Camry. "I'm going over to Perry's house to watch the baseball game with the guys."

"Oh." The *baseball game.* The *guys.* Jeremy didn't bother waiting for an invitation. He knew it wasn't coming.

"You remember Perry? One of my boarding friends."

Jeremy nodded.

"What are you going to do?"

Jeremy dribbled the ball. "Hang out here for a while, I guess. Maybe go watch some TV."

"Liv's upstairs," Patrick said. "Just in case you want to hook up with her while I'm away."

Jeremy sighed. "Patrick, come on. Why are you being like this? How many times can I tell you I'm sorry?"

Patrick got in the car and slammed the door. "As many times as you want. Doesn't mean I'll forgive you." He revved the engine and spun out into the road, leaving Jeremy standing tired and deserted in his dust.

"Dresses on the padded hangers, T-shirts on the top shelves . . ." Liv was organizing her clothes in the armoire late Tuesday night when she heard the front doorbell ring. A few minutes later there was a soft knock on her bedroom door.

"Come in," she called out from behind the door.

"Hi." It was Megan. "I heard about what happened."

Liv sat down on the bed. "Everyone must think I'm pretty awful, huh?"

"No, actually they think you're pretty lucky."

Liv laughed. "Little do they know."

Megan sat down next to her. "I just wanted to tell you that if you need someone to talk to, you can talk to me. I mean, you're alone here without any of your friends or anything, and it must be pretty hard for you."

Liv studied Megan for a moment. "Thanks."

Megan clutched one of the bed pillows. She had an odd, worried look on her face. "I feel kind of funny about something, and I'd feel better if I just spilled it to you instead of you hearing it from somebody else."

Liv lay back. "You're in love with Patrick."

Megan's jaw dropped. "How did you know?"

"A little birdie told me. And besides. I could just tell. You had that look, you know?"

Megan turned a deep shade of red. "I'm sorry, Liv. I—I've liked him for a long time." She touched Liv's shoulder. "But I swear I would never do anything about it. It's just a dumb crush, that's all." She twisted the pillow into a ball. "Are you mad?" she asked in a tiny voice.

"No." Why should she be?

"Well, I didn't want you to hear it from anybody else. But I guess you already did." Megan got up and began to pace back and forth like a panther. "I'm glad that you're working things out with Patrick, really I am." She giggled. "But if things don't work out between you, promise me you'll give me first crack at him?"

Liv laughed. "I promise. But I shouldn't laugh. That might happen. Things have been kind of bleak around here."

"Really?"

"Really." Liv sighed. "I just wish I could go away for a while. Clear my head."

Megan stopped pacing. "You can!" she said suddenly.

"Where?"

"My house. Stay with me for the rest of the week! I know it's not far, but at least you'll be on neutral territory, so to speak." She flopped down on the bed. "Besides, this proves that I really am looking out for your best interest!"

It wasn't a bad idea. "You're sure it'd be okay with your parents?"

"Positive."

Liv stared into the perfectly organized armoire. As hard as she tried, her life just couldn't stay neat and tidy these days.

SEVENTEEN

THE DAYS SEEMED to drag on forever. Ever since Liv had moved out, Pelican's Cove had felt empty. Jeremy felt even emptier. After a week of sleeping in the loft, with only a thin layer of sleeping bag separating him from the hard plywood floor, he'd moved back in the house. The Clarks insisted on it. Actually they had insisted on it after Jeremy had spent just one night in the loft, but Jeremy just couldn't bring himself to move back in. He felt so awkward, so unwanted.

Mr. and Mrs. Clark had been nothing but kind to him. At first they had treated this disaster like it was no big deal. Just some stupid little fight that they'd soon forget, and he and Patrick and Liv would all be the best of friends again in a heartbeat. But after seeing the combination of hurt, anger, and guilt on their faces, the Clarks allowed that it was more serious than they'd realized.

Jeremy had even toyed with the idea of bagging the whole trip and heading back to Erie a week early. But he just couldn't bring himself to leave. It would be like giving up. On Liv. On Patrick. On summer, really.

"Patrick! Jeremy!" Shelby came tearing out onto the deck, where they'd been hanging out, each in their own little world. She pulled off Patrick's headphones. "It's *really* important."

"Don't do that, Shelb," Patrick said sharply, rubbing his ear. "That hurt. What is it?"

"Dad's on the phone. He's down at the marina. He said there's something wrong with the boat . . . he can't get it started or something." She stopped to take a breath. "He wanted me to ask you guys if you could go lend him a hand."

Jeremy folded down the corner of the page he was on and put down his book. "Sure."

Patrick looked over at Jeremy for the first time that day. "Yeah. Whatever. Tell him we just need to put on our shoes and some T-shirts, and we'll bike down in a couple of minutes."

"Okay," said Shelby, dashing back into the house.

"You sure you don't mind?" Patrick asked.

"Not at all."

The Clarks kept their bikes propped along the side of the house. Except for Patrick's, they were all old-fashioned three-speeds. Jeremy had to pedal hard and fast to keep up.

"I wonder what's wrong with the boat," Patrick mused, talking more to himself than to Jeremy. "Dad hasn't had it out for a while. Maybe it just needs to get warmed up."

"Maybe." Having Patrick speak to him again felt so good. Not that they were having a deep conversation or anything. But the past few days had been filled with so many tense moments and angry glances that anything that wasn't made Jeremy optimistic.

The marina was about a mile from Pelican's Cove, accessible either from the street or by the beach. It was an easy bike ride: The terrain was flat, and a special jogging-biking trail led directly to it. After locking their bikes on a bike rack, they spotted Mr. Clark out on one of the docks standing next to the boat. He waved them over.

"Can't figure out what's going on with this old thing," Mr. Clark said, sighing. He ran a hand over the shiny red enamel. "It's not running right. The engine keeps on catching or something. Funny. Never had a problem in the eight years we've had it."

"Does it start?" Patrick asked.

Mr. Clark shook his head. "I've tried to start it three times this morning, but no luck. And I didn't want to get it started and motor out into the water only to have it break down with just me on it." He grinned. "I thought I'd put you two with me in that position."

"Want me to try to start it?" Patrick asked.

"Yeah. Get in." Patrick hopped in.

"You too, Jeremy," Mr. Clark added, patting him on the back. "Go on. Hop in."

Jeremy stepped on the side of the boat and down onto one of the leather seats.

Mr. Clark tossed Patrick the keys. "See if it starts now."

Patrick turned the ignition and the boat started perfectly. He revved the engine. The smell of gasoline trickled through the air.

Mr. Clark began untying the thick brown ropes that held the boat to the dock. "Jeremy. Push off here," he instructed. Jeremy obliged, shoving the boat away from the dock.

"Hurry up, Dad! The boat's going to—" Patrick started.

Mr. Clark stepped backward. "You guys don't need me. Take it for a spin," he called out. "I've got to go talk with somebody inside. See you in a while!" He waved and began walking back up the dock to shore. Then he turned. "Don't come back until you're sure it's running perfectly. It might take a while."

The guys exchanged glances.

"I somehow get the feeling that we've been set up," Jeremy said wryly.

"I'm going to *kill* Shelby," Patrick said with a sigh.

The waters directly off the Beach Haven marina were prime boating areas, for tourists and residents alike. Chartered boats took visitors out for whale watches, and fishermen brought in a daily haul of lobsters and crab to satisfy the high demand in restaurants and local grocery stores.

Patrick let the boat fly across the water, shooting a steady stream of salt water into the boat and on their faces. Normally this would be the kind of thing the two guys would be really into, vying for a chance to steer the boat, daring each other to go faster and faster.

Not today.

Jeremy sat uncomfortably in the seat opposite Patrick's, his arms folded. He tried to enjoy the view of the shore, but the sea spray stung his face, making it impossible.

Patrick stood stiffly at the helm. The boat flew along the water, creating wave after wave in its wake.

People in sailboats are not going to appreciate this, Jeremy thought, noticing a couple of Sunfish swaying in response to the wave impact.

"Maybe you should slow down a bit," Jeremy offered.

"I know what I'm doing," Patrick answered icily.

Jeremy shrugged. The boat slammed into the waves, each bang sending a thump onto the boat. He swallowed. They couldn't go on like this. Not only did he suspect things between Patrick and Liv were bad, his friendship with Patrick was going downhill fast. Total disintegration.

"It's cool, going for a boat ride," Jeremy offered. "We should have done this a few days ago. Liv told me . . ." He trailed off. *Why don't you be a total moron, Jeremy? Pass me the salt, so I can rub a little more in Patrick's wounds.*

Patrick's hands tightened on the wheel. "Yeah, well, I was planning on taking you and *Liv* out here for a boat ride. But my plans kind of got changed on me."

The leather seat under Jeremy's legs felt hot and sticky. Slowly he lifted one leg. It made a gentle sucking sound as he did. He repositioned himself and took a deep breath.

"Patrick? I think we should talk about what happened." He gave his knuckles a sharp crack.

"What?" Patrick asked, stepping on the gas. "I can't hear you." The increased speed made the wind sound even louder. "What was that you were saying?"

"I was saying that I think we need to talk," Jeremy said, trying to talk over the wind. He was practically shouting now.

"Oh, sorry. I thought that was you talking, Jeremy. It was a little gnat, buzzing in my ears." Patrick took a hand off the wheel and flicked the imaginary bug away. "There. It's dead now." He wiped his hand dramatically on his shorts and gave Jeremy a fake smile.

Jeremy shook his head and stared out into the water. He knew he was the one to blame. He'd always known that. But if Patrick wasn't even willing to talk to him, nothing could ever bring them close again.

Jeremy sighed. Could he blame Patrick for feeling as he did? Not really. He had every right in the world to be angry. Furious.

The Clarks had meant well, trying to get them out here alone together. But it wasn't working.

A "broken" engine was easy to fix.

Broken trust wasn't.

On their way back to their bikes Jeremy and Patrick passed a volleyball net. A trio of guys were volleying the ball back and forth. One of them, a tall, muscular redhead, served the ball hard at his opponent, a dark-haired, gorilla-faced guy. He missed, and the ball sailed over and stopped at Patrick's feet.

He picked it up and lobbed it back over. "Those guys are such jerks," Patrick said under his breath.

"Yeah?"

Patrick shook his head. "They're always doing stupid stuff, like playing catch with a real baseball on the beach. Or deciding to play water polo right where we're boarding. Intelligent stuff like that."

The redhead who'd caught the ball jogged over to the edge of the court. His eyes drifted over the two of them. "Nice shorts, Clark," he said, gesturing to Patrick's oversize aqua trunks.

"Thanks, Pawley. I thought so too," Patrick said coolly. He and Jeremy kept walking.

"You guys having a picnic together out there?" yelled Gorilla Face. "It looked cozy." He and his friends snickered.

"You're a real comedian, Santangelo. You should go on *Leno*."

He laughed, a goofy, toothy snicker. "Yeah. Maybe I should."

"So. You two wusses want to play? Or are you off to get to know each other better?" said Pawley. This drew a big round of laughter.

Jeremy looked them over. He could tell they were idiots before they'd even opened their mouths. They just had that moron look about them. He shot a glance at Patrick.

"Are you thinking what I'm thinking?" he asked, the lure of competition stirring up the old camaraderie they'd shared for so long.

"Yeah." Patrick nodded. They turned around. "We'll play," he called as they walked back. "Two on two."

"Which one of us are you afraid to play against?" asked the third guy. He too was tall, with droopy blond hair and a snaggle-toothed grin.

"Doesn't matter to us," said Jeremy. "Let's just play. You can serve first."

The blond guy parked himself at the side of the court. "I'll ref."

"Give us a couple minutes to warm up," Patrick called.

Jeremy leaned down beside him, touching his toes. Then he rose and gave his legs a good shaking out.

"Let's kill them," Patrick muttered under his breath.

"Sounds good to me." Jeremy stood up. *Whack.* The volleyball smacked him squarely in the face.

"Whoops," said Pawley, pretending to be upset. "I thought you were ready."

Patrick grabbed the ball and stepped back to the right corner. "We are now," he said grimly.

Jeremy tossed the ball in the air with his left hand and hit it hard with his right fist. He and Patrick had won the first match, 15–11. Now they were trailing, 12–13. His ball went flying over the net firm and fast before his opponents could react.

"Ace!" yelled Patrick, shooting Jeremy a grin. "Thirteen–thirteen."

Jeremy served again, slamming the ball as hard as he could.

Santangelo leaped awkwardly into the air, attacking the ball with a vengeance. He managed to make a block, sending the ball back hard.

Patrick threw himself on the ground, going for the dig. The ball flew up seconds before it hit the sand, falling neatly on the other side.

"Wake up, Santangelo!" Pawley cried. "Are you sleeping out here?"

"That was your ball," Santangelo spat.

Patrick leaned forward, his hair soaking with sweat. "Are we playing or having a party?" he said, motioning for them to give him the ball.

Santangelo flung it under the net.

"Fourteen–thirteen," called Jeremy. "Game point." He sent it easily over the net. Pawley threw himself at the ball, spiking it right back. The ball headed straight for Patrick.

Patrick got under the ball and acted as setter, bumping it to Jeremy, who jumped up and spiked the ball over the net. Pawley and Santangelo lunged for it, but the angle was impossible to defend. The ball came to a stop in the sand.

"All right!" Patrick yelled, leaping up and giving Jeremy a high five.

Jeremy grinned, high fiving him back. "That was a pretty sweet setup."

"Thanks for the game, guys," Patrick said as he and Jeremy picked up their discarded T-shirts and headed back down the beach. "Anytime you need a little workout, just give us a call."

Jeremy laughed as he heard the guys muttering and swearing to each other. "That was pretty awesome, Clark," he said as they jogged down to the water to cool off.

Patrick grinned back. "That it was, Thomas."

And for a moment, it was as if the incident with Liv had never happened. It was forgotten. Pushed aside. And what really mattered had managed to find its way to the surface.

But then a dark shadow crossed Patrick's face, and Jeremy knew that the memory of what he had done had crawled back into Patrick's head once more. It had felt so good to have his best friend back, if only for a little while. Natural. How it was supposed to be.

The boat trip had been a waste. But the game had proved something. Their friendship wasn't gone. It was strong once. It could be strong again.

A guy could hope, right?

They unchained their bikes and rode the rest of the way home in hot, sweaty silence.

EIGHTEEN

J EREMY STOOD IN the shower, letting the hot, soothing water pelt down on his neck and shoulders. They ached from the workout he'd had earlier. "That was some game," he muttered to himself, still pumped from the volleyball match that afternoon. "We showed those losers."

As he shampooed his hair he realized there was something oddly familiar about the shampoo. It smelled like Liv. He squinted down at the label. She must have left it in the shower by accident. He worked the shampoo into a lather, letting the soapy, flowery foam drip down his neck. The smell made him sad. Funny how smells could do that. Since they'd arrived, it had happened before—that a scent triggered a memory. Mrs. Clark's aromatic tomato sauce reminded him of his own mom's tangy blend. The sheets he slept on had a clean, fresh smell, like his own back home. And the scent of the salty

191

ocean air and of wet beach towels and swimsuits always made him think of summer. But this shampoo didn't make him happy.

It reeked. Of smiles and tears. Of cool summer breezes and unexpected laughter. Of linen. Of earrings and anklets.

Of Liv.

Jeremy blasted the cold water on his head, washing away the shampoo residue.

He knew now. He guessed he'd known all along. But the game today really proved it.

He couldn't give up on Patrick. Patrick had been his friend practically forever. He was more than a friend. He was his ally against the world. Always there for him, through good times and bad.

And this admittedly was pretty bad. But as bad as it was and as angry as Patrick had been, Jeremy had seen something today that he hadn't seen since the big blowup.

For the first time all week Patrick had given him respect.

And that, Jeremy realized, was everything. He didn't respect himself for what he had done. For how he had acted. But he could change things. He could try.

As he towel-dried his body he heard a little thump outside the bathroom door. He wrapped the towel around his waist and opened the door. Biscuit stood there, her tail wagging happily. She barked in greeting.

"Just you and me, Biscuit," Jeremy said, giving

the dog a scratch behind her ears. She barked and tore off down the stairs. He pulled on a pair of jeans and a white T-shirt. He was on his own tonight. Mr. and Mrs. Clark were out to dinner with friends, Shelby was spending the night with Mallory, and Patrick was out with Liv.

He wondered what they were doing. How they were getting along. He felt so lonely. Making things right with Patrick was something he had to do . . . but he still couldn't bring himself to say he'd given up on Liv.

He sighed as he threw his dirty clothes in his duffel bag in the guest room. It was definitely too much to think about on this, the last weekend of the summer.

The last weekend of the summer . . . a news bulletin in Jeremy's head went off. Tonight was Friday . . . the night of the big fight on HBO. It wouldn't be a total downer after all. He could hang out in the family room, have some chips and soda, watch the fight, and put off the misery of friendship and romance until tomorrow.

He thumped down the stairs and into the family room. A light shone out from the doorway. Mrs. Clark must have left it on to make him feel more comfortable. To his surprise, the TV was on too . . . and he wasn't alone. There, sprawled out on the comfortable old couch, was Patrick.

"Heard you singing up there. Nice tune."

"I, uh, thought I was alone here," Jeremy mumbled. "Weren't you going out with Liv tonight?"

"Yeah. We were going to. But I didn't really feel up to it. I kind of felt just like lying here. Being a slob." He grabbed a handful of buttery popcorn from a large ceramic bowl. "The fight's on tonight. I almost forgot, with all the crap going on lately."

"Is she here?"

"No. She went to Atlantic City with Joyce and her parents. They went to see some show at the Taj Mahal."

"Oh."

A commercial for underarm deodorant flashed on the TV. "Mind if I join you?" Jeremy asked. It was weird to actually be having a conversation with Patrick after the silent treatment of the past week.

Patrick gestured to the overstuffed armchair next to him. "Be my guest."

Jeremy sat down, resting his arms on his knees. The fight wasn't going to start for another hour or so. Plenty of time for uncomfortable silences to occur. "What's this?" He picked up a dog-eared scrapbook off the wooden coffee table. "Your mom's sketchbook or something?"

"No. It's my scrapbook of us. Pictures and stuff. Things I've collected over the years."

Patrick had kept a scrapbook of them? Of their friendship? Who said guys weren't sensitive? This was a surprise. Jeremy held it unopened in front of him, unsure. "Can I, I mean, uh, is it okay if I look at it?"

"Yeah. Sure." Patrick shrugged. "There's some funny stuff in there, let me tell you. I was cracking myself up before you came downstairs."

"Yeah?" Jeremy flipped through the first pages. There was little tow-haired Patrick, toothless and grinning in the first grade, surrounded by a group of other toothless kids. And in second grade, posing with his teacher in front of the blackboard.

"Hey, look at this," Jeremy exclaimed. It was a picture of him and Jeremy, standing outside Jeremy's front steps in front of a pile of boxes. They had their arms slung around each other.

"That's the day you moved in," Patrick said, leaning over to look at the photo. "The day we first met."

Jeremy shook his head in disbelief. "I can't believe you have a picture of that."

"That's nothing. Check out the rest of it."

"Look at us here!" Jeremy howled. A small blond cowboy, dressed in a suede vest, jodhpurs, and felt cowboy hat, stood arm in arm with Frankenstein, complete with a squared-off head, scarred face, and dark suit.

"That was a cool costume," Patrick reminded him. "I remember how you scared those girls dressed in the princess costumes. They were really freaked out."

"Those were the days." Jeremy turned the page. "Wow. Look how small we were." It was their Little League team picture.

"We thought we were so big. Remember that game against the Mariners, when we were what? Nine? Ten?"

Jeremy put his legs up on the table. "How could I forget? You pitched a no-hitter! It totally

195

annihilated their winning streak. They hated you."

Patrick smiled. "I was convinced I was destined for baseball greatness."

"Weren't we all."

The pages were covered with sports memorabilia: Patrick in each year's Little League uniform. Then Midget Football. Rugby. And soccer. And always, right by his side, was Jeremy.

"I can't believe you kept this," Jeremy said, pointing to an old ticket stub. It was faded, but you could still make out the words. The New York Mets at the Pittsburgh Pirates. Saturday, June 2. 1:00 p.m. "That was my first ever baseball game. I remember Mitchell being mad that I got to go to a game for the first time the same time he did."

"Of course I kept it. It was my first game too."

Jeremy laughed. "What is *this?*"

"Remind me to never let my mother dress me again," Patrick moaned, pointing to a picture where he looked like a cross between a Scottish piper and an escapee from a plaid pants factory.

"As long as you remind me never to get a crew cut again."

"Deal," Patrick said. They shook hands.

Through good pictures and goofy ones, Jeremy noticed that one thing above all stood out from the album.

In every picture they looked happy. Like they were having the time of their lives. *We were having the time of our lives,* Jeremy realized. *Just hanging out and being friends.*

They finished flipping through the album. A few pictures of girls had cropped up: Patrick and Jeremy with girls at a junior-high dance, Patrick with a different girl at the ninth-grade class picnic.

Girls could come and go.

But Jeremy and Patrick had a history. Something worth preserving.

"Look, Patrick, I'm sorry." There. He'd said it. For the past hour they'd been reminiscing, focusing on all the good times. But all along the problem was still there.

Patrick pulled down the throw that rested on top of the couch and began toying with the fringe. He said nothing.

Jeremy swallowed. "I was wrong. I never should have done what I did. I know you hate me now. But I hope that—" He broke off and stared at the floor. He couldn't bring himself to look Patrick in the eye. "Patrick, I know you probably don't believe this, but I never meant for anything like this to happen. It's just that there was something . . ." He struggled to put it into words. "Something there with Liv. Something I'd never felt before. I went after it." His voice cracked. "I think I could have fallen in love with her if I'd let myself. If she'd let me," he amended. "But I could have never been with her if it meant destroying everything with you. You've gotta believe that."

Slowly Jeremy lifted his eyes. Patrick sat, staring out the window toward the sea.

"Hate you?" Patrick shook his head. "I don't hate you, Jeremy."

"Well, you—"

"I hate what you did to our friendship. And yeah, you basically shattered what I thought was the best relationship I was ever going to have." Patrick held his hands in the air. "But I could never hate you."

A feeling of intense relief rushed over Jeremy. Patrick hadn't written off their friendship. *He doesn't hate me. After what I did, he doesn't hate me.* Jeremy felt tears welling up in his eyes. Great. That was all he needed, to sit here crying like a girl in front of Patrick.

"When I walked in and saw you kissing Liv, I wanted to *kill* you. I mean, I couldn't believe what I was seeing. It was like a bad dream, or a movie that's happening to someone else. Except it wasn't happening to someone else, and it was starring me, you, and Liv." Patrick threw some unpopped kernels back into the bowl. "I didn't want to believe it. I can't even tell you what I was thinking. It's like a giant blur."

"I felt the same way, if you can believe that," Jeremy said.

Patrick grabbed another handful of popcorn. "I've done some serious thinking over the past week. And I'm starting to think that maybe you did me a favor."

"Huh?"

"Well, the more I thought about it, I realized what really made me mad had everything to do with Liv and nothing to do with her. It was basically all about me and you. I felt like if I was betrayed by the one person I'd counted on my whole life, how could I trust anyone again?"

"Patrick, I—"

"Let me finish. Don't you see what a problem that is?" He stopped. "Look. Liv has everything I've ever wanted in a girlfriend. She's beautiful, smart, funny. But you know I've never managed to stay with one girl for very long."

Jeremy nodded.

"With Liv, though, it was different. She wasn't dragging me down. But being here this summer got me thinking. I got defensive last week when you commented about all the girls on the beach I know, but the more I thought about it, it's true." Patrick gave a small laugh. "I *do* know a lot of girls. I like girls. A lot. And I started to find myself wanting to see what other girls were like. I guess I was just fooling myself by saying a carefree night at the movies or a walk to the ice cream shop was nothing. I mean, it was nothing, but it was something all the same." He stopped. "Am I making any sense?"

"I think what you're trying to say is the phrase girls everywhere hate. You're afraid of commitment."

Patrick began to nod. "Yeah, in a nutshell. But when I thought about what an awesome girl I had in Liv, I thought I must be nuts to give her up for something unknown."

"You felt comfortable with her."

"Yeah. But it was more than that. I really, really

like her, Jeremy. You know that." He stood up and began to pace.

"I know," Jeremy said quietly. There was no denying the pain in Patrick's voice.

"And knowing that you knew made the fact that you'd go after her really hard for me to deal with." His voice was low. "I couldn't believe you'd do something to hurt me."

Jeremy rubbed his temples. "I was so caught up in Liv that I didn't think about the consequences until it was too late. I—I don't know what else to say."

"You fell for Liv. I can understand that. I did too. But I also realized that I could really, really like Taylor. And Didi. And Claire."

"And Megan," Jeremy finished.

"Megan?" Patrick got a funny look on his face, as if Jeremy had unearthed some big secret. "She's special, you know? I never really got to know her before this summer, but we spent some time hanging out, and she's pretty cool. Yeah. Megan's definitely someone I could go for."

"See, that's the difference between you and me," Jeremy said. "You can like a lot of people. But I can't. When I find someone I like, it's all or nothing."

"And you honestly thought you found that with Liv."

"Yeah," Jeremy answered truthfully. "But if it's not cool between us, it could never work between Liv and me. And Liv was pretty clear about her choice in boyfriends."

Patrick walked over to the glass doors and

opened them. A rush of air blew in the room. He turned suddenly.

"It's okay, Jeremy. Do what you have to. And whatever that is, I'll be all right. Liv and I—we're through."

Jeremy's jaw dropped. "You guys broke up?"

"You could say that."

Jeremy sat there for a few moments, drinking it all in. What a night. He walked over and held out his hand to Patrick. Patrick shook it. He didn't say a word.

"So are we friends again?" Jeremy asked hesitantly. The sound of Liv's chimes rang softly in the cool ocean breeze.

"We always were," Patrick told him.

NINETEEN

"I'M GOING TO miss you, Liv," Megan said dejectedly. "I wish we didn't live so far away from each other." They were sitting in the plush lounge chairs on Megan's deck, watching the beach go by.

Things were beginning to wind down in Beach Haven. Summer families were packing up, kids were beginning to think about school once more, and local merchants were reluctantly saying goodbye, selling their souvenirs at half price.

"We can always write," Liv told her. "It'd be cool to hear what's going on in Philadelphia."

"One of my dad's college roommates lives in Erie," Megan said thoughtfully. "Maybe we'll come visit."

"Maybe I'll be back next year," Liv said. Then she made a face. "Then again, maybe I won't be invited."

Megan laughed. "You're always welcome here."

"Thanks." Liv smiled.

From the beach below they heard the *clap, clap* of sandals against the wooden stairs. Two heads, one blond, one brunette, appeared.

"Hey," said Patrick.

Jeremy came up behind him. "Hi, girls."

"Hi," they answered.

Liv couldn't *believe* that the two guys were actually standing next to each other without being at each other's throats. They actually looked . . . happy. Suddenly she knew that what she was going to say, although difficult, was the only thing she *could* say.

"I need to talk with you," Liv told Patrick after giving Jeremy a quick glance.

"Good," Patrick said, following her down the stairs and onto the beach. "Because I need to talk to you."

"This is a cute place." Liv twirled slowly around on the old-fashioned rope swing. She and Patrick had walked down to the small playground that sat adjacent to the beach. A few kids ran around, but the park was pretty much deserted. There were a few swings, some seesaws, and an old rickety slide, all covered with a light dusting of sand.

"I used to bring Shelby here all the time. She's outgrown it now," Patrick said, giving the slide a rap. He took a seat on the swing next to Liv.

She scuffed her gym shoes in the sandy dirt. "I guess people outgrow things after a while." Liv held on to the rope tightly, the scratchy twine digging into her skin. "Like we did." She'd known that this conversation was coming. It was inevitable.

Patrick turned his swing to face her. "We had some great times together."

"Yeah." Liv's stomach fluttered at the memories.

Patrick leaned forward. A lock of blond hair fell in front of his eyes. Liv resisted the urge to push it back.

"You know, if this thing with Jeremy hadn't happened, we'd still be going out now," Patrick reflected. "But we'd have broken up sooner or later."

"You think?"

"Mm-hmm. Jeremy and I had a long talk the other night. He made me realize I don't want a steady girlfriend right now. No offense to you. You were great. Are great," he corrected. "In fact, you're so great, you definitely would have gotten sick of a beach bum like me."

Liv let go of the ropes, spinning around and around. "Don't be so sure." She paused. "I loved being your girlfriend, Patrick. But when Jeremy and I met, it—"

Patrick held up his hand. "I don't need to know the details."

Ouch. Liv leaned forward. "We never meant to hurt you. I hope you know that."

Patrick nodded. "You did, though. I can't lie. But me and Jeremy, we're cool again. And if you guys think you've got something, then . . . go for it."

Liv felt as if the world had just been lifted from her shoulders. She felt deliriously happy. *Patrick and Jeremy are friends again. Patrick doesn't hate me. And . . . Jeremy and I are a couple.*

Quietly Patrick took Liv's hand in his tan one, rubbing his finger across her palm. "I know I'll have other girlfriends. But you'll always be my first love, Liv."

Liv's knees began to shake. For a moment the thought that maybe she was making a terrible mistake crossed her mind. But she knew she wasn't. What she and Patrick had had was incredible. But their relationship was over.

"And you're mine," she said, meaning every word. And for the first time in days, when Patrick moved in to hug her, it felt right.

"Are you ready to go home?" Megan asked, joining Jeremy at the deck's railing.

"No. Not really." He grinned. "But I don't think I have a choice in the matter." Time had functioned on its own wacky cycle for the past two weeks. Speeding up. Slowing down. Dragging forever and then disappearing before he had the chance to capture it.

He watched as Liv and Patrick made their way down the beach. He felt so different than he had a week ago . . . waiting for Liv and Patrick to return after the big bombshell had been dropped.

From a distance he saw the pink dress that was Liv turn around. She stopped, her long hair blowing back in the wind. He wasn't sure, but he thought he saw the white flash of her smile. Patrick's too.

Two people were determining his fate.

And Jeremy had a feeling his future was looking pretty good.

"I love the beach at night," Liv murmured quietly, leaning back, resting her head on Jeremy's shoulder.

"Me too." He wrapped his arms around her, softly kissing the top of her head.

Dusk was slowly turning into night. The faint sounds of some dreamy summer song drifted down the beach. It was the last party of the summer—the last time for a long time that the teenagers on the beach would have the chance to laugh and talk, to do things with the carefree abandon that only summer can provide.

Jeremy sighed contentedly. How things had changed from two weeks ago. Liv and Patrick had broken up, and now Jeremy was holding Liv in his arms.

"They really look happy together," Liv said, nuzzling her cheek next to Jeremy's.

Jeremy spotted Patrick and Megan, standing off to the side. Megan's arms were outstretched as if she was in the middle of some big story, and her face was all lit up. Patrick seemed to be listening intently.

"I'm glad," Jeremy said, giving Liv's head another kiss. "I hope you are too."

Liv twisted her neck around. "Do you have to ask?" They kissed then, softly. All the guilt, all the furtiveness was gone. And in its place was trust. Trust in each other. In the decision they had made.

In their future, whatever it might bring.

Jeremy's fingers felt the smooth metal surface of the heart pendant, hanging on its silver chain around Liv's neck. He'd given it to her at sunset, when they'd walked out to the sea, letting their toes get tickled by the waves. And it was a thank-you, in its own way. A thank-you for her love.

"I gave you my heart tonight, Liv," he murmured.

"And I'm never giving it back," she whispered.

The sound of the surf, the smell of the sea, the feel of the sand . . . Jeremy never wanted it to end. And as he held Liv in his arms, he knew that it wouldn't. Every time he looked at Liv, the memories of this time, this place, this summer would come flooding back.

It was a summer he'd never forget.

The summer that he fell in love for the very first time.

The Reliability Quiz

Every girl wants to find the perfect guy, but once you've captured his heart, how do you make it last? Trust is a big part of any good relationship, but it's something that's earned over time. You have to find out if you can rely on your guy to do the little things before you can trust him with your heart. Take Jenny and Jake's special love quiz to see if *your* boyfriend is trustworthy.

1. Before homeroom, your boyfriend decides to go back to his locker to fetch a textbook. You ask him to grab the science homework you left in your locker. When he comes back, he:

A. Has your science homework safely tucked in his backpack.
B. Has your science homework . . . but it's covered with chocolate fingerprints from the doughnut he was eating.
C. Has his textbook, a half eaten apple, his gym clothes, his Discman, and no science homework.

2. He says he'll pick you up at 5 o'clock—when the football game he's catching on TV is over. At five, the game is in overtime. Your boyfriend:

A. Calls and asks if it's okay to pick you up after the game has actually finished.
B. Shows up after triple overtime, over an hour late, and never calls.
C. Shows up at 5 o'clock anyway. He wouldn't dare keep you waiting.

3. Your printer isn't working and you have a term paper due the next day. Your boyfriend agrees to print it for you and bring it to school the next day. When your teacher asks for the work, you:

A. Have it ready to go: printed, spell-checked, and neatly stapled.
B. Have to tell her your printer died but your forgetful boyfriend promised he would go home at lunch and print it out.
C. Ask for an extension. Your boyfriend erased the disk and saved the new info he downloaded from an *X-Files* website.

4. The two of you spend one evening staring up at the stars and discussing your dreams for the future. You tell him that when you were little you dreamed of becoming a belly dancer. He takes this information and:

A. Tells his mom because he thinks it's so cute.
B. Never breathes a word. He's happy you told him such a fond secret.
C. Announces it at the lunch table the next day and asks you to get up to do an exhibition dance for the crowd.

5. It's Valentine's Day and you're excited to see what your guy has in store for you. You get to school and find:

A. A rose in your locker, a box of candy on your desk, and an invitation to a great restaurant that night.
B. A blank look on your boyfriend's face. "It's Valentine's Day . . . already?"
C. A note taped to your locker that says "Happy Valentine's Day! Sorry I forgot your gift but I'll make it up to you at dinner tonight. Be my Valentine?"

6. You go to all of his football games and cheer your heart out. This weekend you're starting goalie in your soccer game for the first time this season. He:

A. Is there for every save, cheering until he's hoarse.
B. Shows up late but leads the crowd in cheers for the entire second half.
C. Calls you that night and tells you he couldn't make it because the guys wanted to get burgers after practice.

7. You see your boyfriend talking to a pretty girl at his locker. When you ask him about it later, he tells you:

A. She's a girl from his math class who wanted to borrow his notes.
B. The same as A—adding that you have no reason to be jealous. You're the one he loves.
C. Girl? What girl? You must have been seeing things.

8. *The two of you are watching your little brother on a Saturday afternoon. Your parents call and ask you to come pick them up because their car has broken down. Your boyfriend offers to watch your brother so you don't have to load the car seat. When you return with your parents:*

A. Your brother is crying in the playpen and your boyfriend is in your room listening to Pearl Jam.
B. Your boyfriend is giving the baby his bottle and watching *Sesame Street*.
C. They're both asleep on the couch.

9. *He finally agrees to see a romantic movie with you. When you get to the theater, a girl in the ticket line waves to your boyfriend, and then whispers something to her friend. Your boyfriend:*

A. Shrugs and tells you she's no one important.
B. Says, "She wasn't waving at me," and then quickly ushers you inside.
C. Tells you he went out on a date with her last year but only liked her as a friend.

10. *You tell him, in absolute secrecy, that your best girl-friend has a crush on his best guy-friend. His friend:*

A. Is pumping you for details in a nanosecond.
B. Comes to you about a week later and asks you what's going on.
C. Will never know.

SCORING:

1. A—2, B—1, C—0
2. A—1, B—0, C—2
3. A—2, B—1, C—0
4. A—1, B—2, C—0
5. A—2, B—0, C—1
6. A—2, B—1, C—0
7. A—1, B—2, C—0
8. A—0, B—2, C—1
9. A—1, B—0, C—2
10. A—0, B—1, C—2

THE VERDICT

If your score is between 0 & 7:

You've got some major thinking to do about this relationship! Your boyfriend is one of two things: either a complete scatterbrain, or totally self-centered. Either way, *you're* the one who's suffering. If he's really important to you, talk to him and let him know that you feel as if he doesn't really listen to you. He doesn't seem to have enough respect for your feelings or even for your stuff. Point out a couple of instances, like when he left your art project on a hot stove, or when he answered the phone while you were in the bathroom and never gave you the message. Maybe he'll change his ways. But if not, you should let this guy go, or live to regret it.

If your score is between 8 & 14:

Your guy messes up every once in a while, but it could be that he's just being a guy. Often, certain things seem monumentally important to girls, while the same things wouldn't be given a second thought by a guy. Valentine's Day, for example, was not invented for men. Some guys realize it's important to their girlfriends, but others honestly don't see the point. The idea is, when your boyfriend does something that hurts your feelings, seems irresponsible, or negatively affects your life, let him know. Hopefully he'll clean up his act, and become totally worthy of your trust.

If your score is between 15 & 20:

Well my dear, you have found perfection . . . or have you? Is your boyfriend just being trustworthy and caring, or is he letting his life revolve around you? If he spends all of his time making sure your life is perfect, you may feel like a pampered princess. But what about his life? Sooner or later he'll realize that he's not doing anything for himself and he may begin to resent you. When this happens, it's never pretty. Don't get angry if he wants to spend time with his friends every once in a while. What would you do if you didn't have chat time with your pals? Give him some space, and you may live happily ever after.

Do you ever wonder about falling in love? About members of the opposite sex? Do you need a little friendly advice but have no one to turn to? Well, that's where we come in . . . Jenny and Jake. Send us those questions you're dying to ask, and we'll give you the straight scoop on life and love in the nineties.

DEAR JAKE

Q: *This summer at camp I flipped head over heels for this great guy named Jon. We always hung out together in this big group of friends. He spent most of the summer dating a girl named Amanda, but he always treated me as if I was special. We would have long talks about school and relationships and the future. It seemed like all he ever did with Amanda was flirt and stuff, so I always hoped he would realize I was the one for him. Now we're home and Jon lives nearby, but Amanda lives in another state. I keep wondering if I should call him or write to him. What do you think?*

DA, Waukegan, IL

A: Go for it, girl! Of course you should get in touch with him. Why not? You guys were obviously friends, so he won't think it's weird if you call him. And if Amanda lives so far away, it's possible that the great "out of sight, out of mind" rule will apply.

With her out of the picture, he could take one look at you and realize what he was missing all summer. Of course, you don't know that for sure, but what do you have to lose by getting in touch with him? Absolutely nothing. In a case like this, there is no reason not to take the chance. And even if nothing romantic happens, at least you can continue the friendship you began over the summer.

DEAR JENNY

Q: *This guy, Keith, followed me around like a puppy dog for almost a year. When he realized I wasn't interested, he started hanging around with my best friend. Then I got jealous, probably because of the whole "you always want what you can't have" theory. So I started calling Keith all the time, and he finally asked me out and I said yes. But now I realize that he's really just a good friend. I don't feel anything more than that, and I don't know what to do. I have to break up with him, but I feel so guilty. Help!*
TW, Kissimmee, FL

A: Getting tricked by jealousy never feels very good. I understand why you feel guilty. Keith probably feels great that he finally got what he wanted after a year of trying. But you can't let that stop you from being happy. If you stay with him, you'll just begin to resent him and resent yourself for settling for someone who's not right for you. Sooner or later, Keith will catch on to the fact that you're not very excited about being with him, and then a number of things can happen. Either he'll start wondering what's wrong with him because he can't keep his girlfriend interested, or he'll start trying to change or do more and it will only make you feel worse. You don't want to put a friend through that. Keith probably wouldn't want to be with someone who wasn't totally into him anyway. You both deserve better.

Do you have questions about love? Write to:

Jenny Burgess or Jake Korman
c/o Daniel Weiss Associates
33 West 17th Street
New York, NY 10011